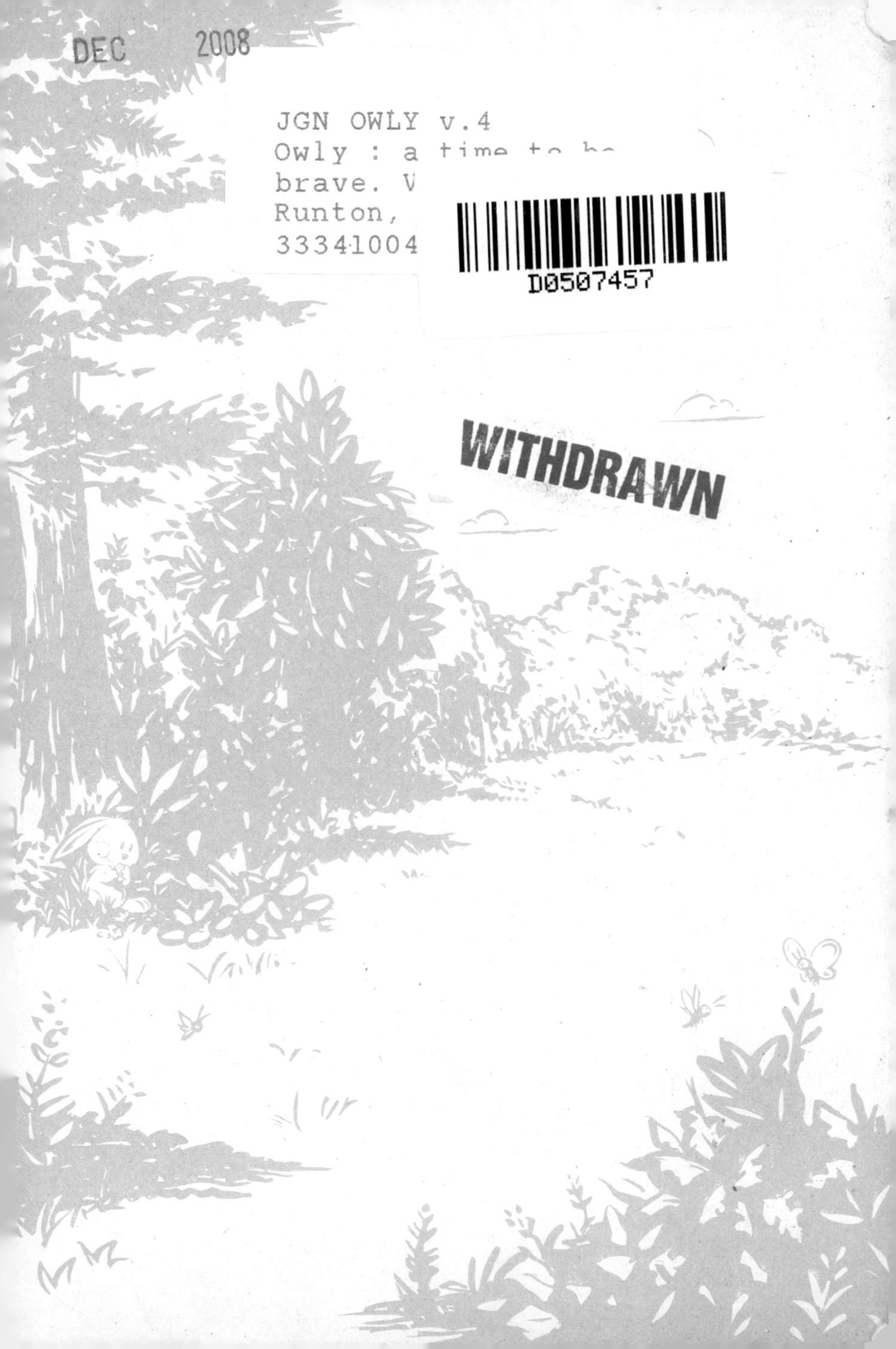

OWLY™

A TIME TO BE BRAVE

ANDY RUNTON

OWLY:
VOLUME FOUR, A TIME TO BE BRAVE
© 2007 ANDY RUNTON

OWLY IS™ & © 2003-2007 ANDY RUNTON

ISBN: 978-1-891830-89-1

1. ALL-AGES
2. ORNITHOLOGY
3. GRAPHIC NOVELS

TOP SHELF PRODUCTIONS
P.O. BOX 1282
MARIETTA, GA 30061-1282
U.S.A.

WWW.TOPSHELFCOMIX.COM/OWLY

PUBLISHED BY TOP SHELF PRODUCTIONS, INC.
PUBLISHERS: CHRIS STAROS AND BRETT WARNOCK.
TOP SHELF PRODUCTIONS ® AND THE TOP SHELF LOGO ARE
REGISTERED TRADEMARKS OF TOP SHELF PRODUCTIONS, INC.

EDITED BY CHRIS STAROS & ROBERT VENDITTI

TREE FRIENDLY!
PRINTED ON RECYCLED PAPER
FIRST PRINTING, DECEMBER 2007
PRINTED IN CANADA

WWW.ANDYRUNTON.COM

FOR PRINCESS GALE
FOR HELPING ME TO BEGIN WRITING
MY VERY OWN FAIRY TALE.

AND FOR MY MOM ALONG WITH MY
FRIENDS, FAMILY, AND ALL OF THE OWLY FANS
FOR THEIR ENCOURAGEMENT, KINDNESS,
SUPPORT, AND ESPECIALLY... PATIENCE.

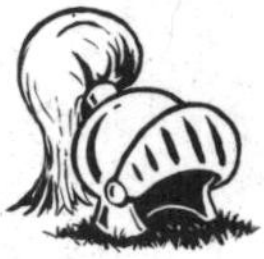

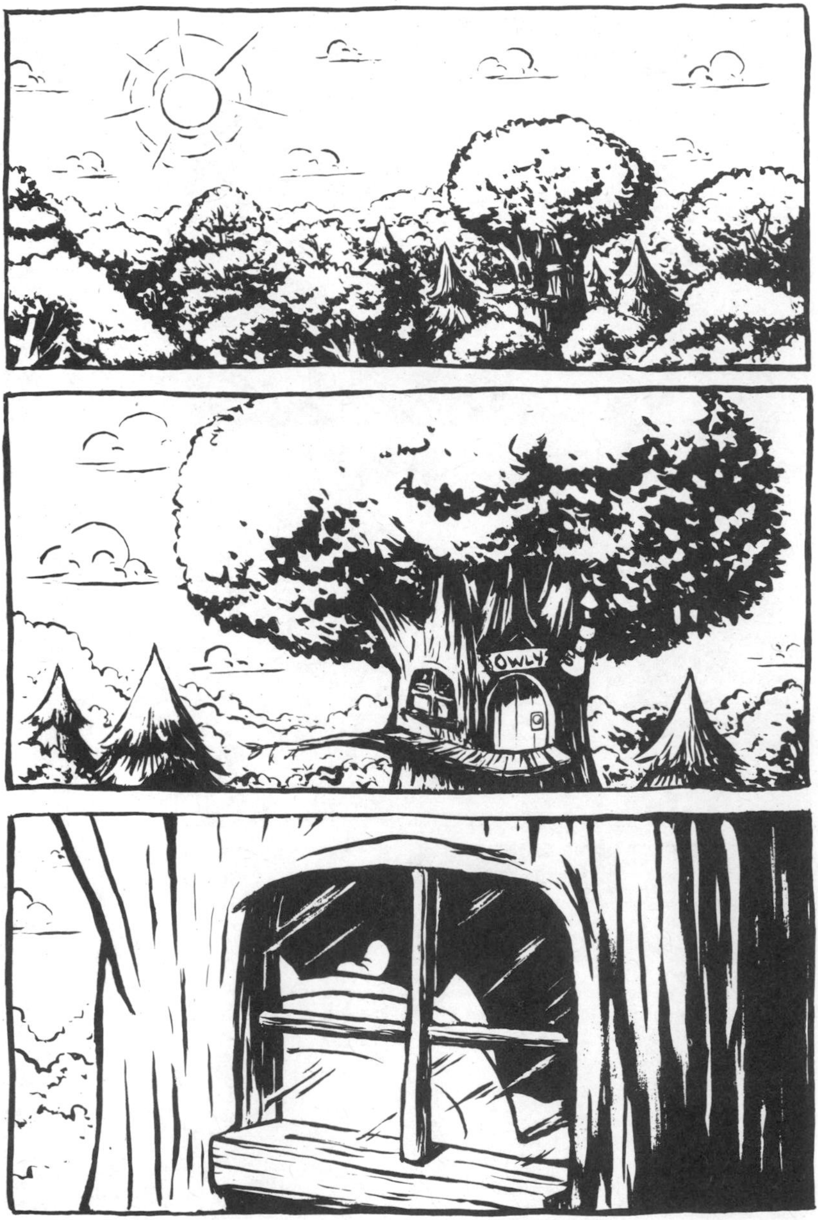
OWLY

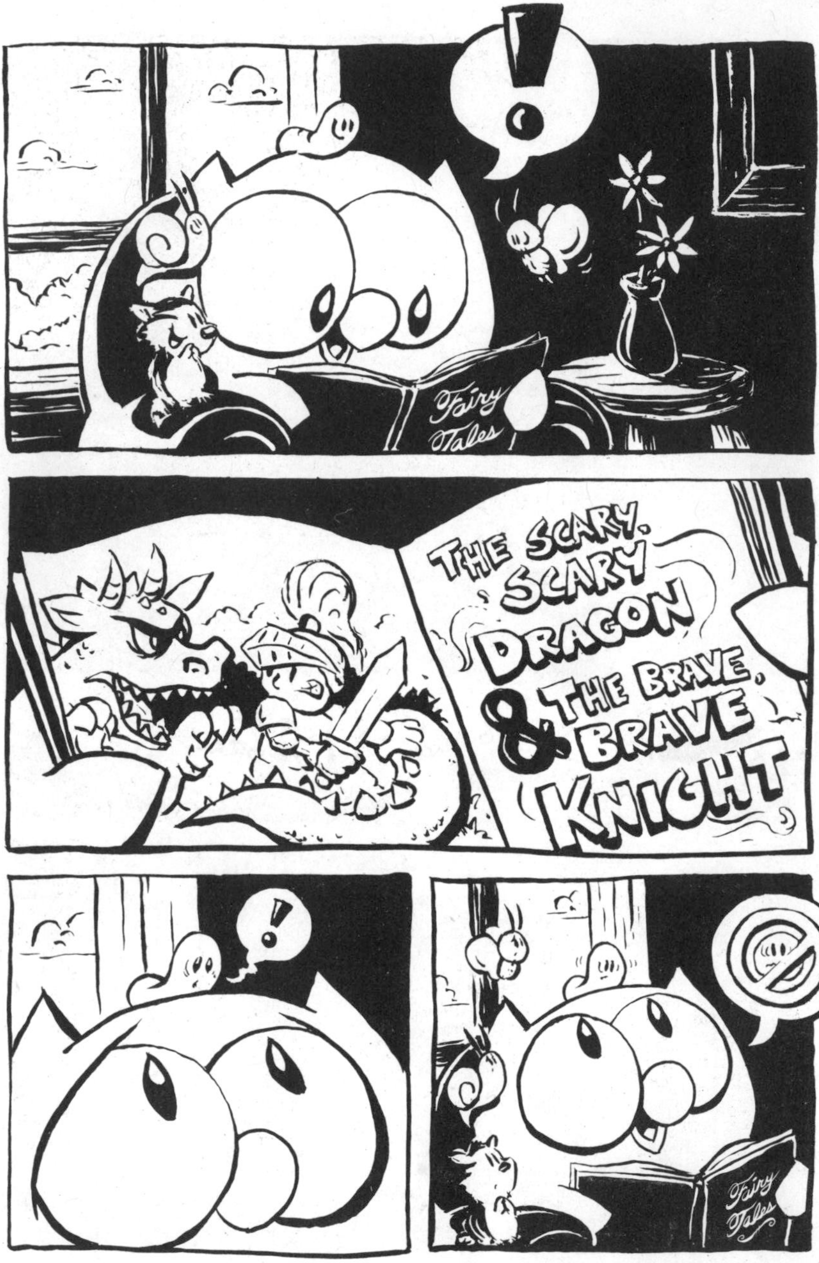
!
Fairy Tales
THE SCARY, SCARY DRAGON & THE BRAVE, BRAVE KNIGHT
!
Fairy Tales

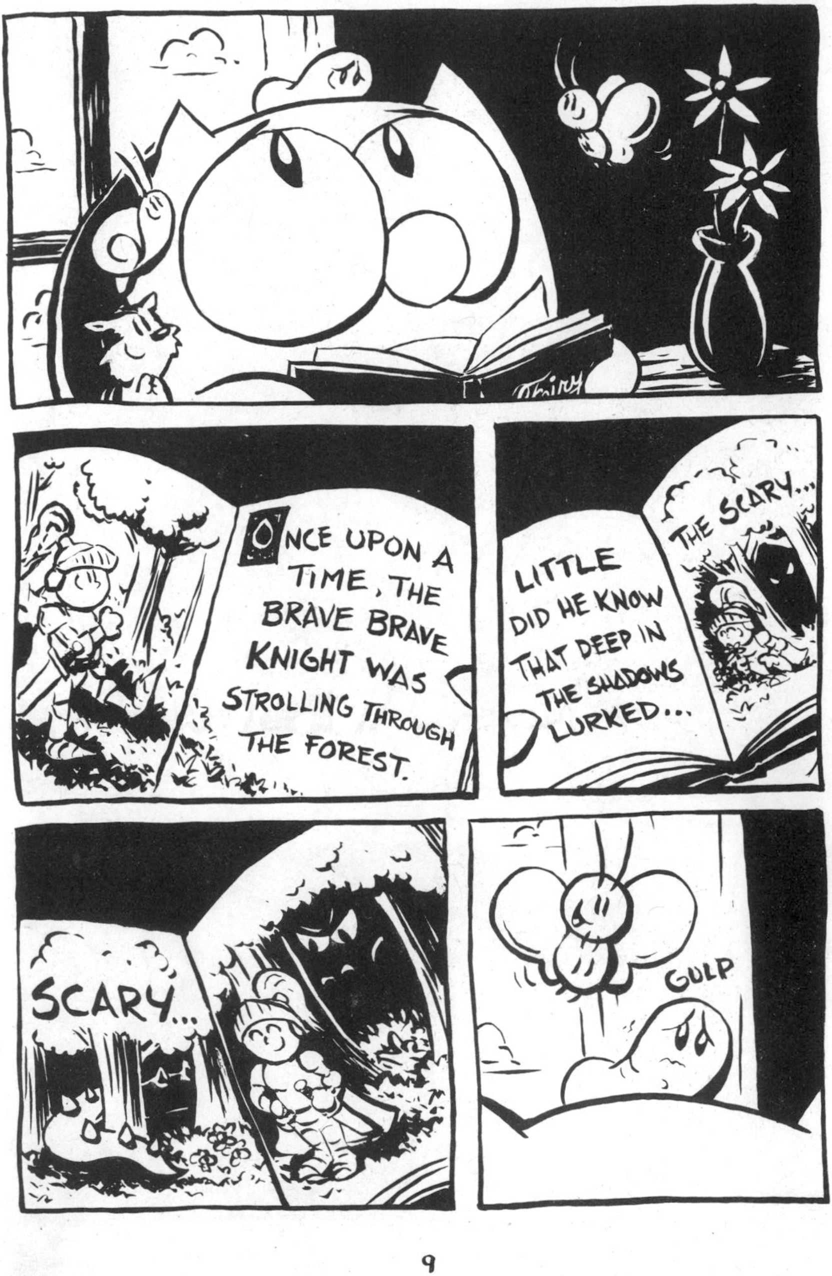

Once upon a time, the brave brave knight was strolling through the forest.
Little did he know that deep in the shadows lurked...
The scary...
Scary...
GULP

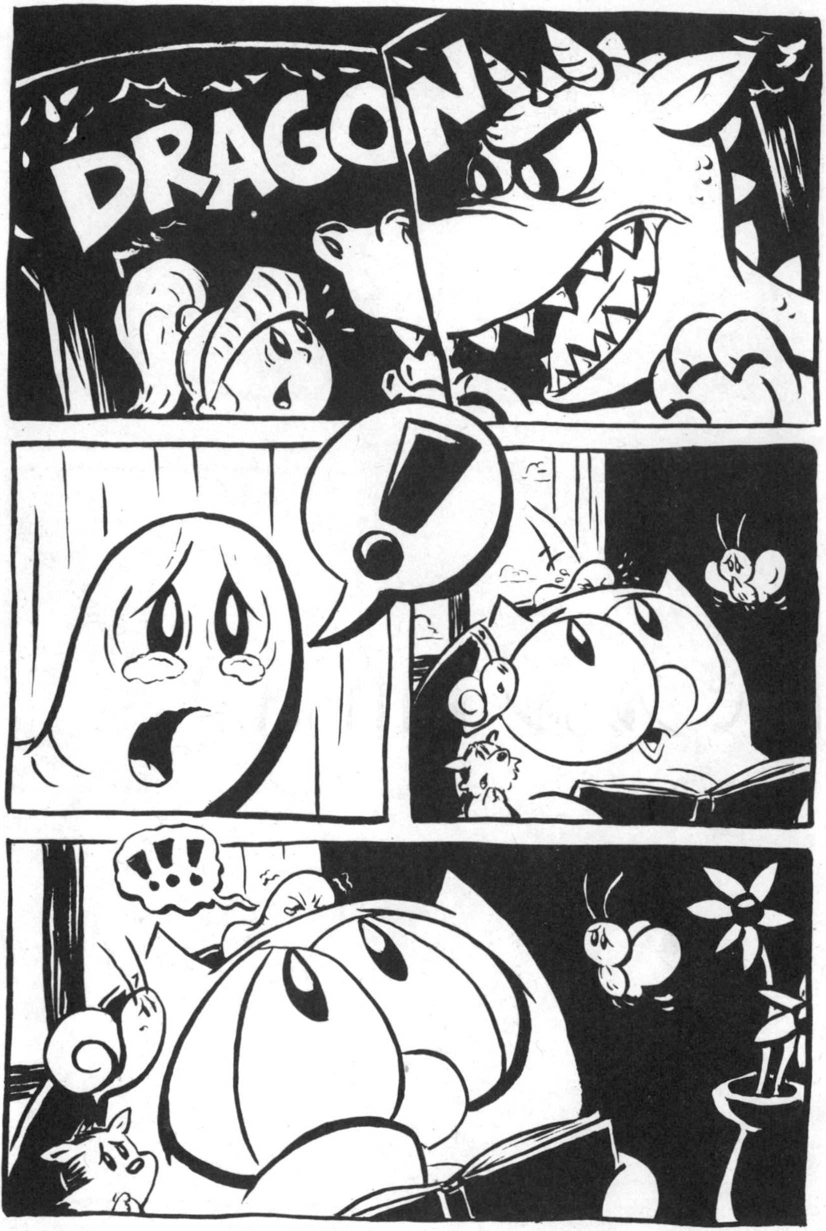
DRAGON
!
!!!

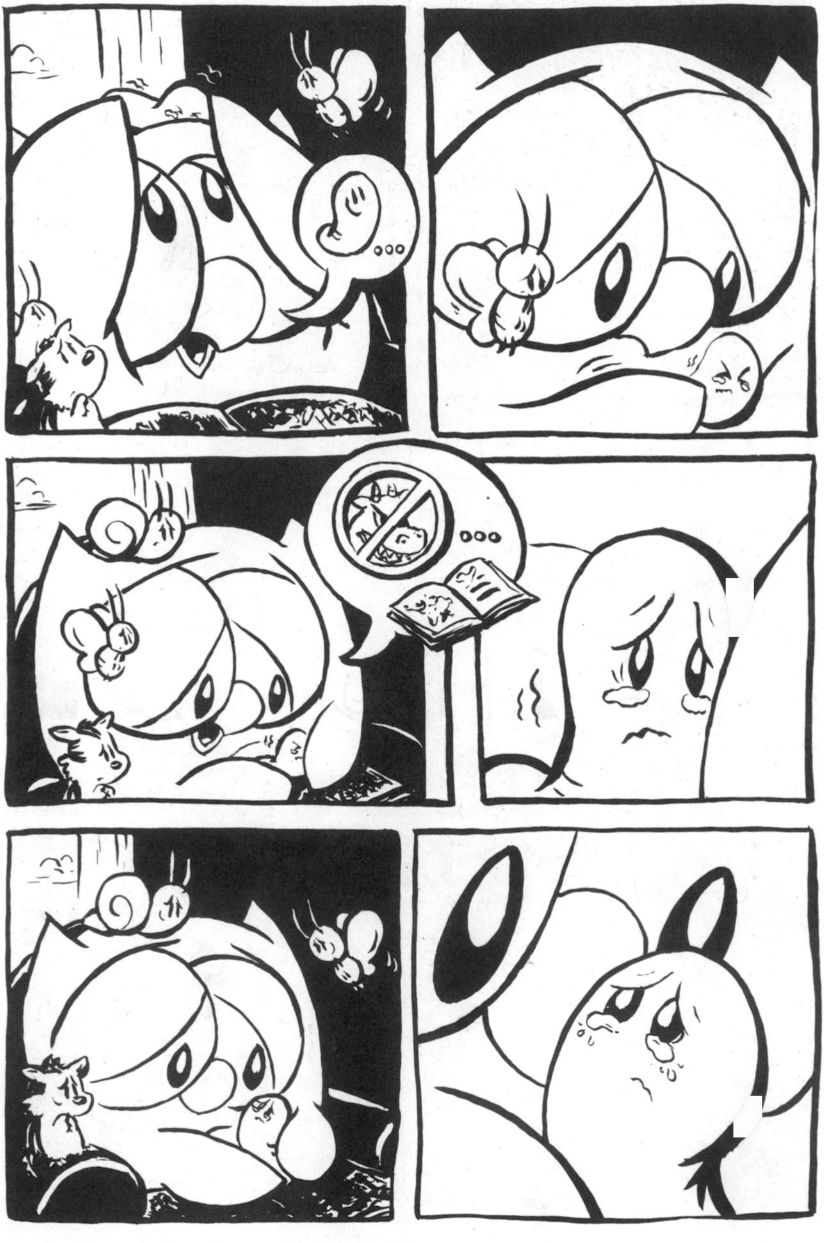

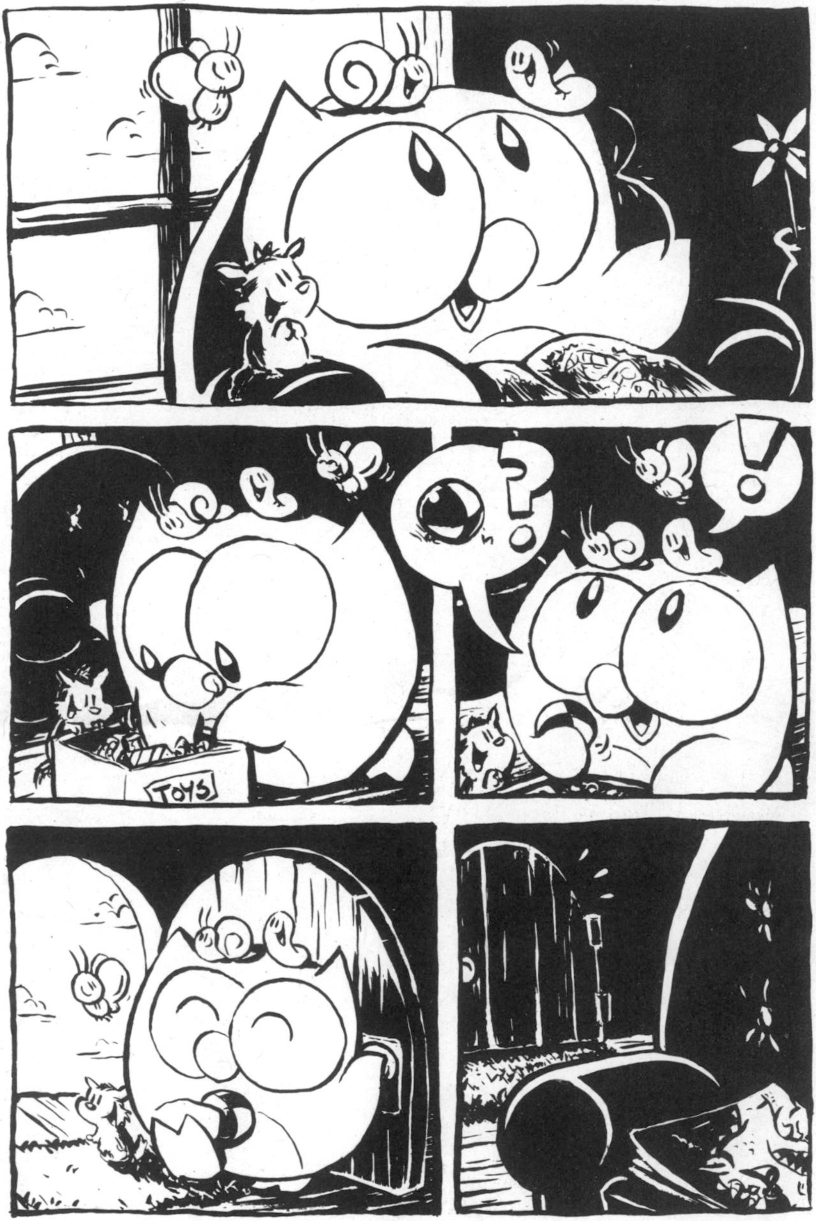
?
!
TOYS

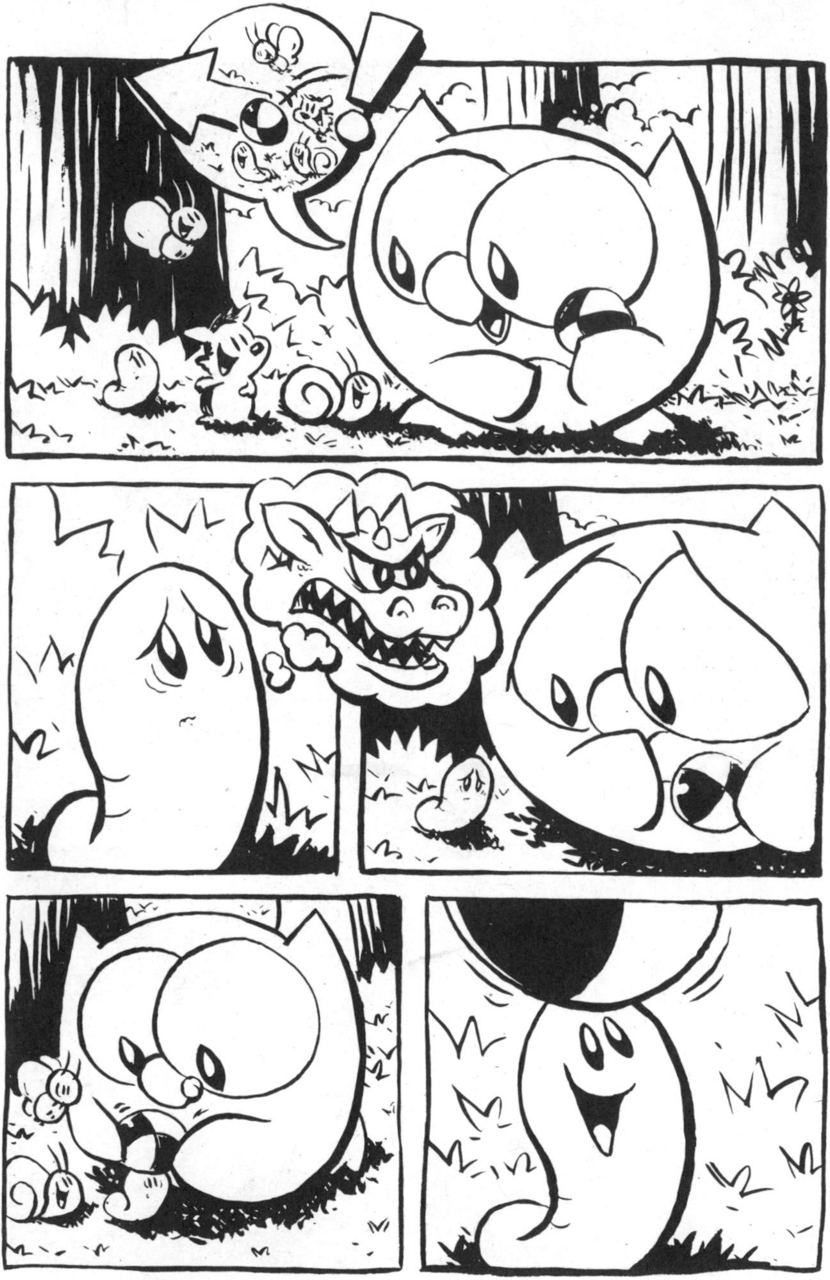

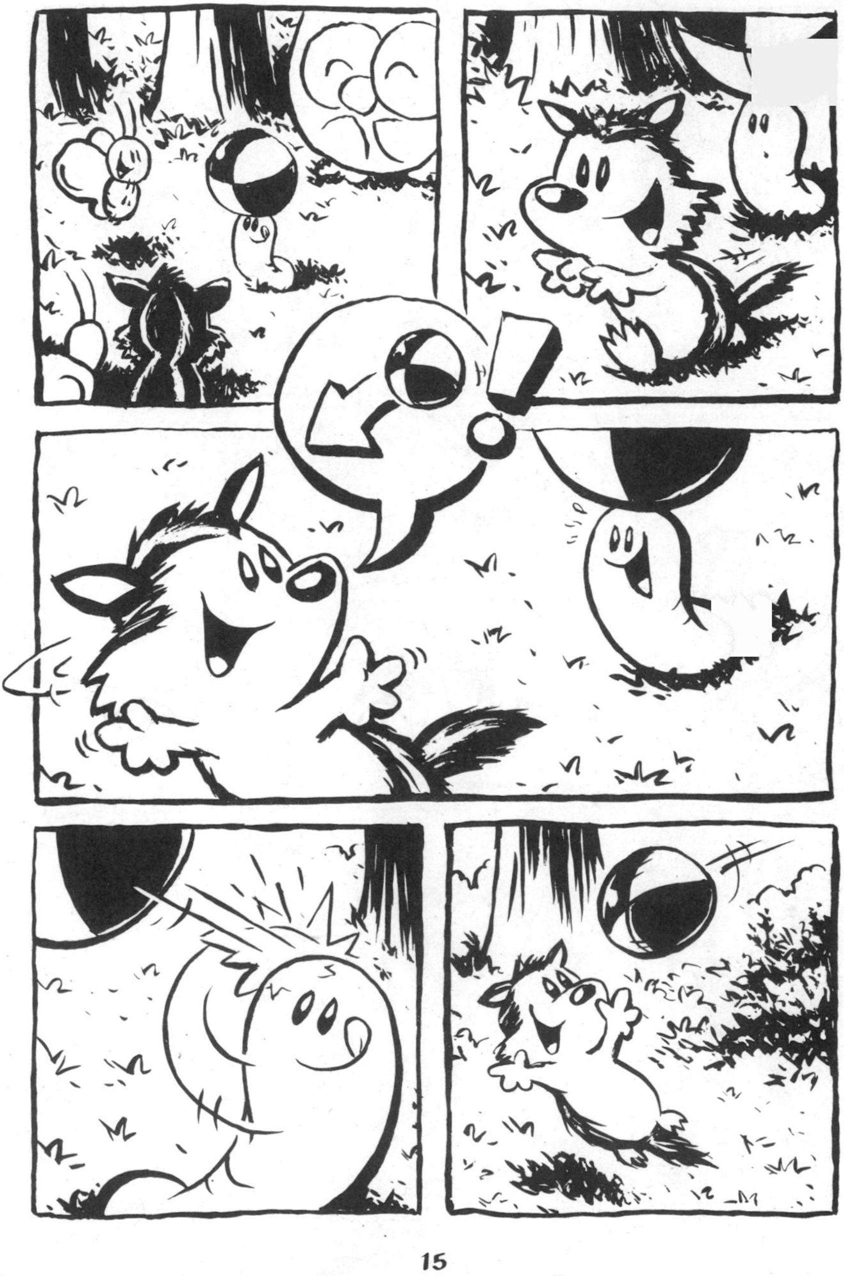
!

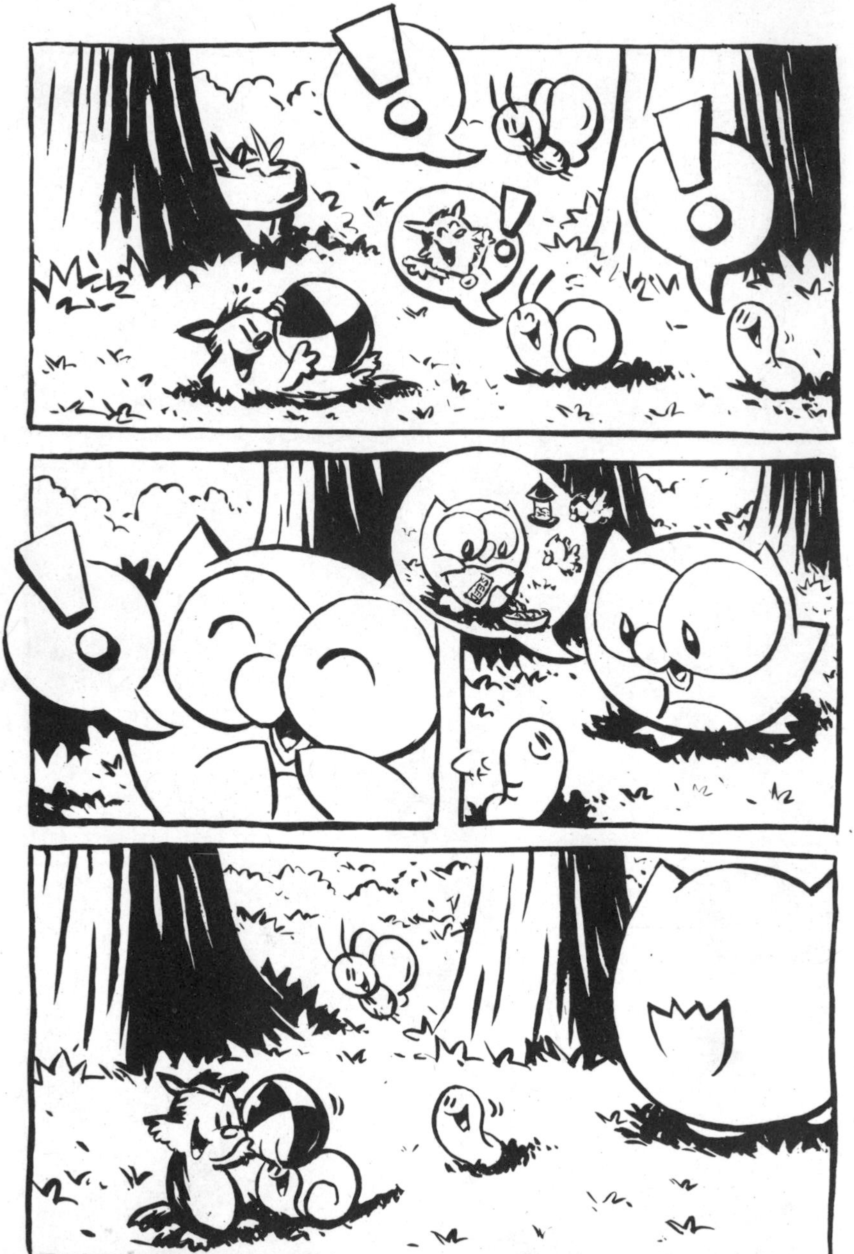
!
!
!
!

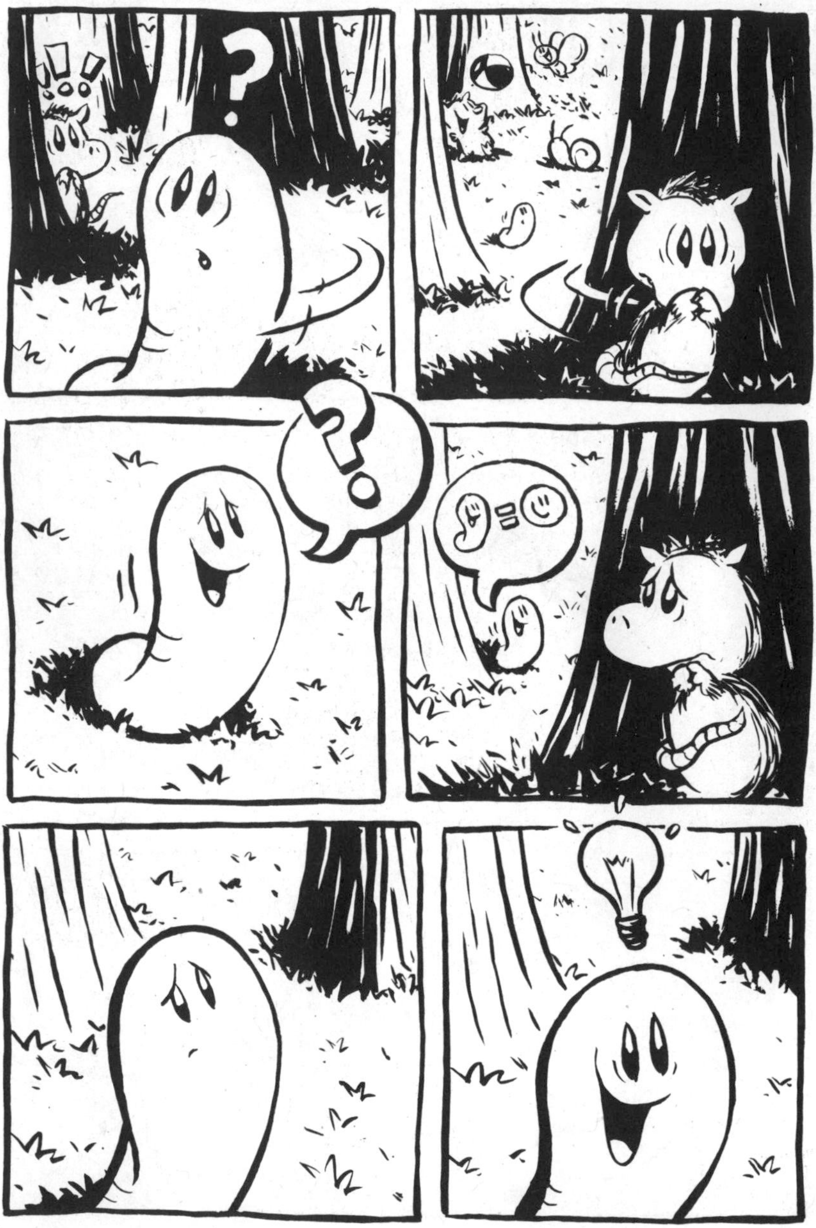

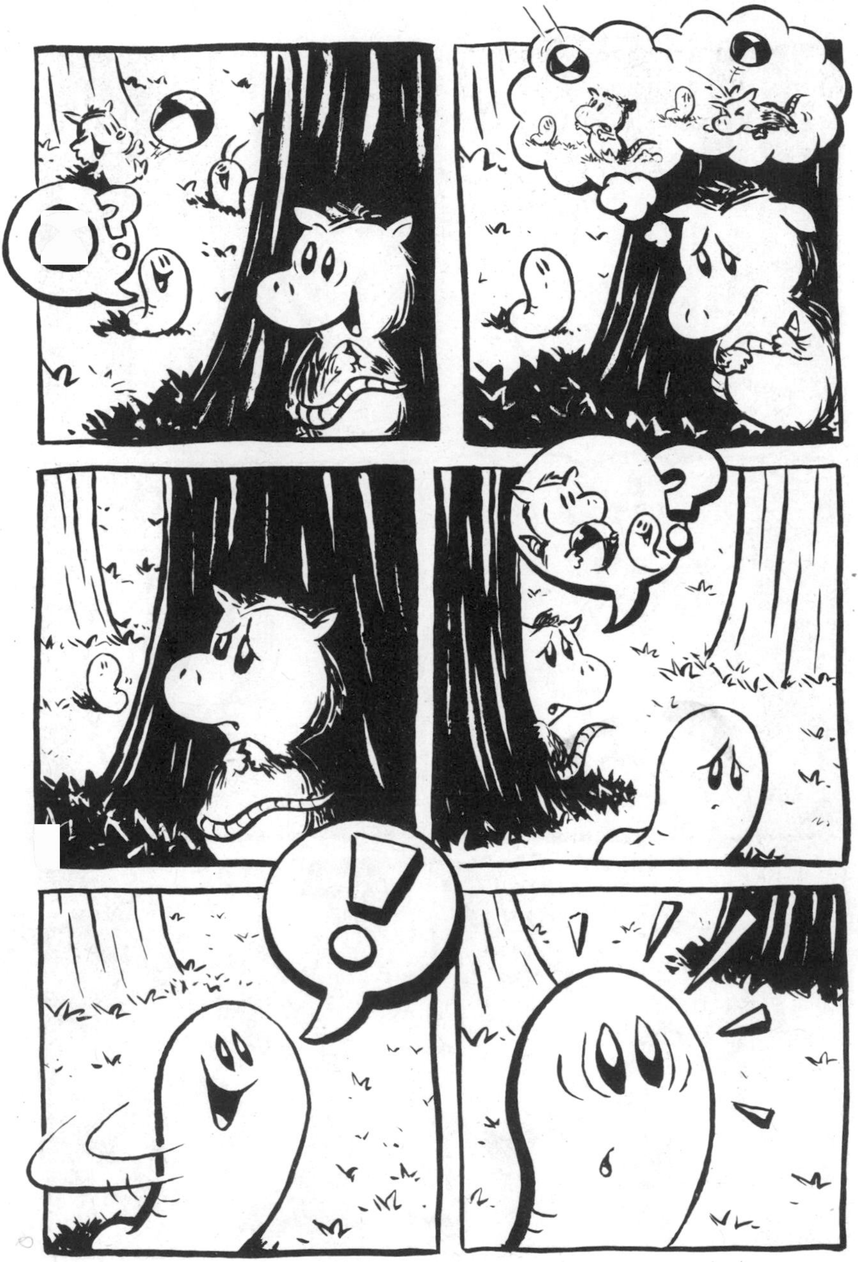
?
?
!

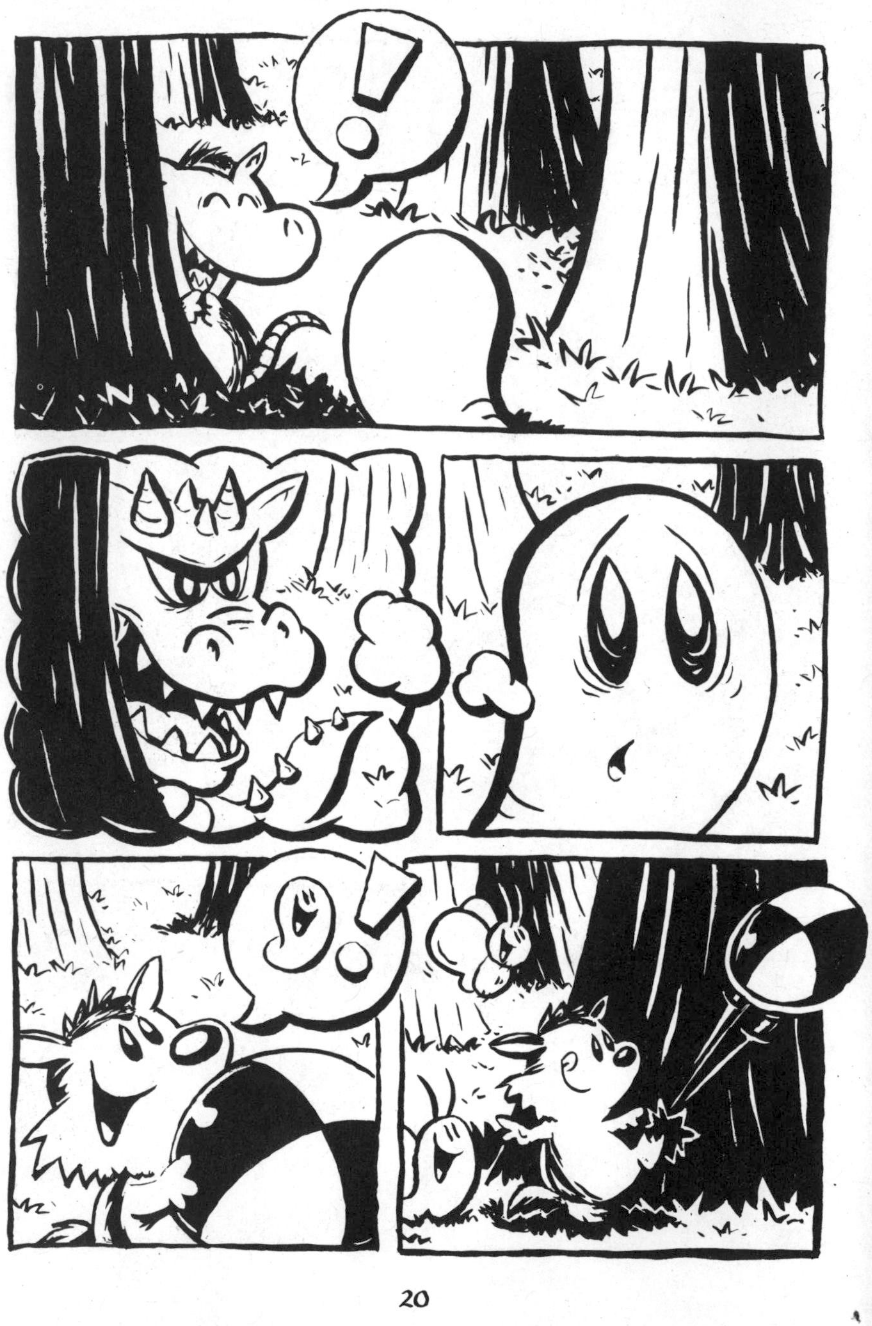
!
!

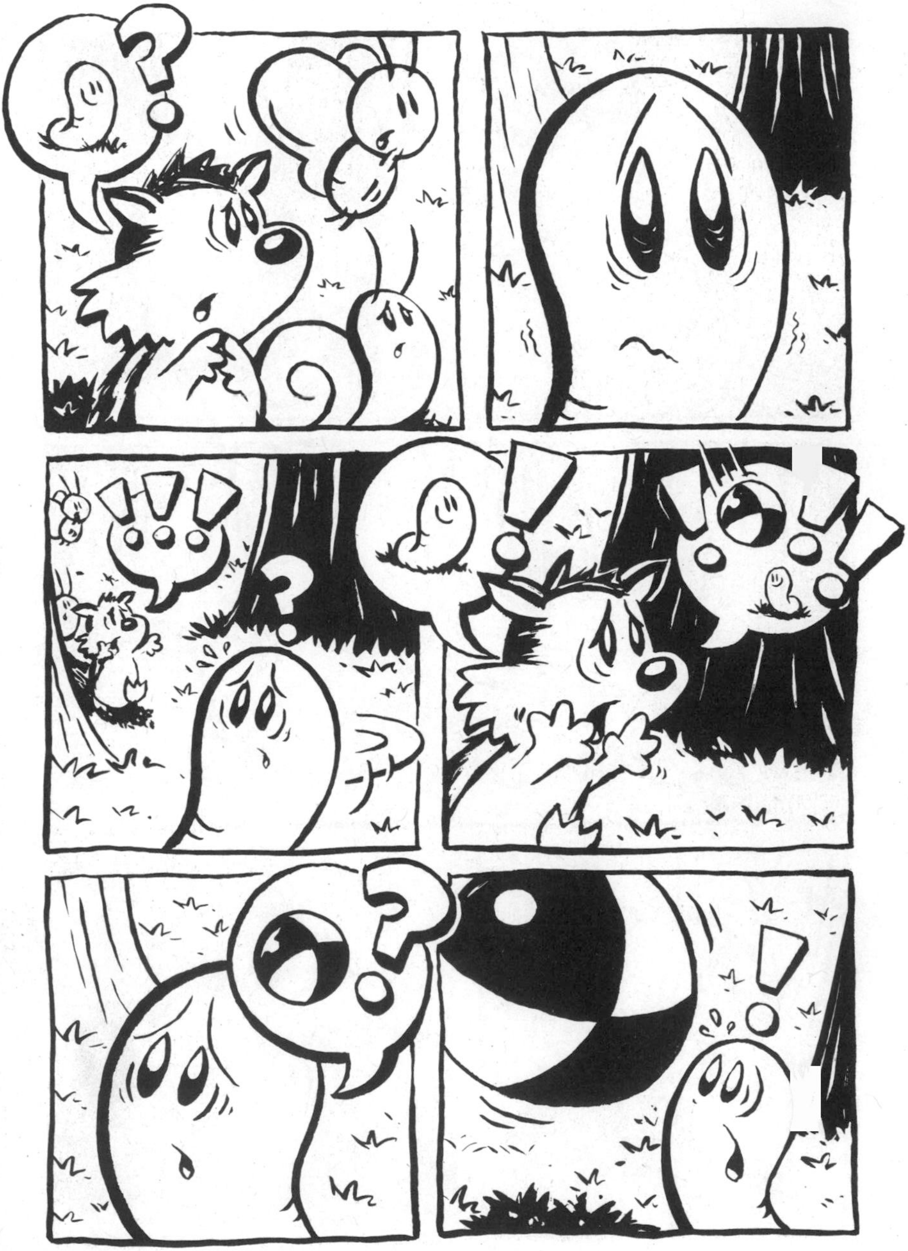

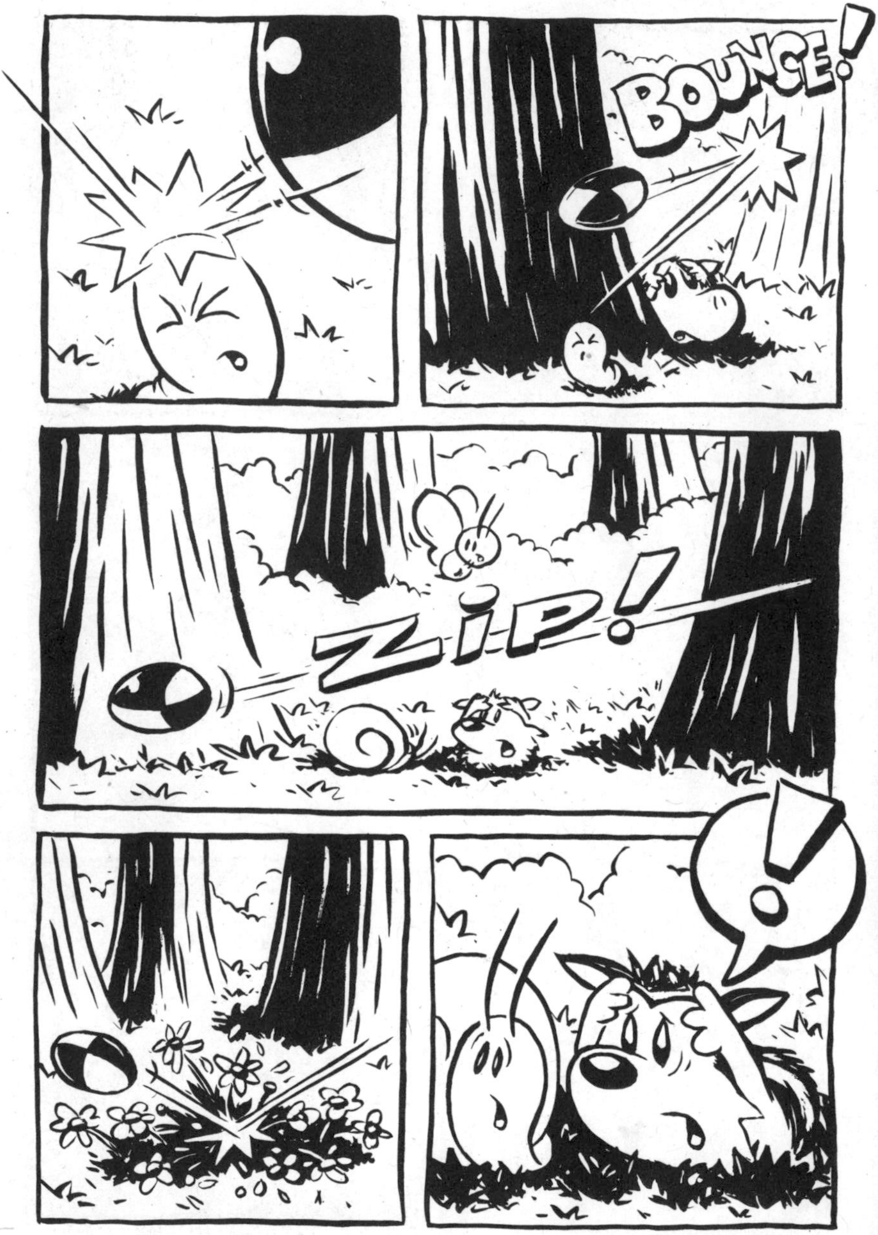
BOUNCE!
ZIP!
!

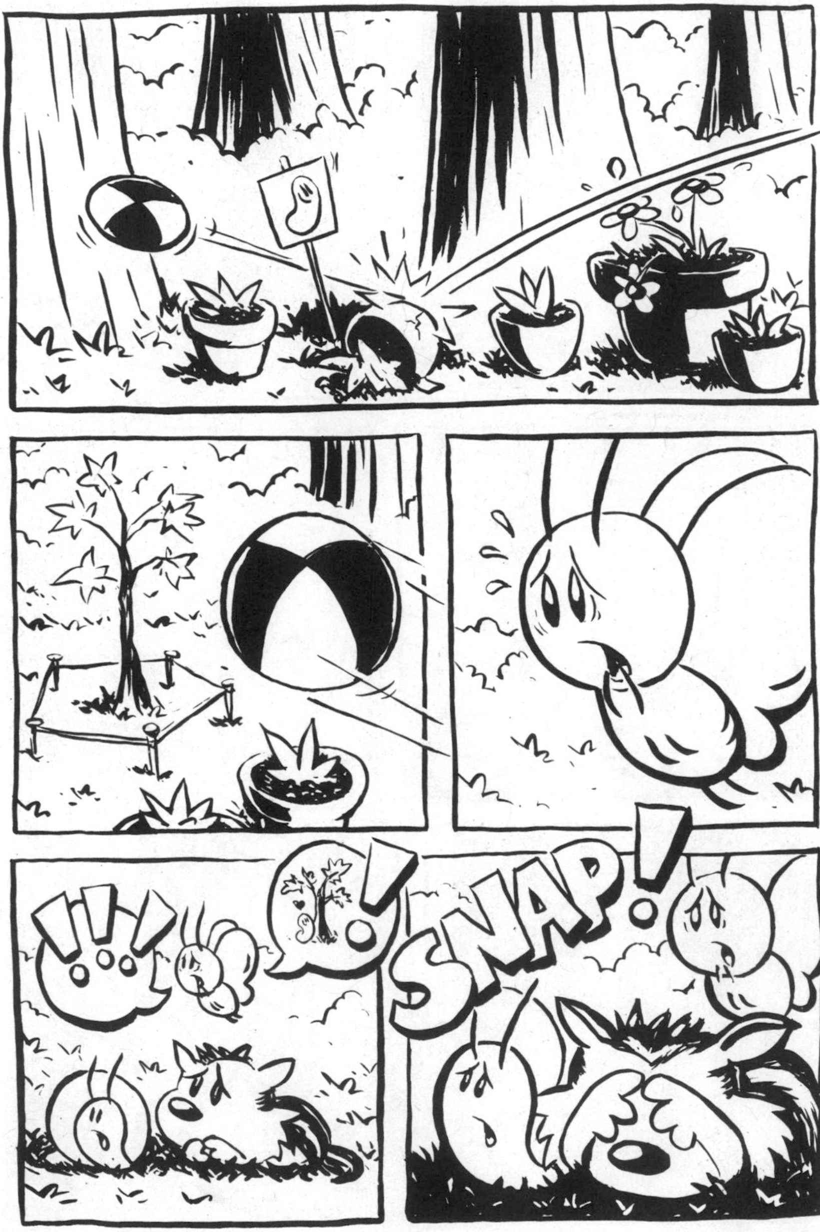
!!!
SNAP!

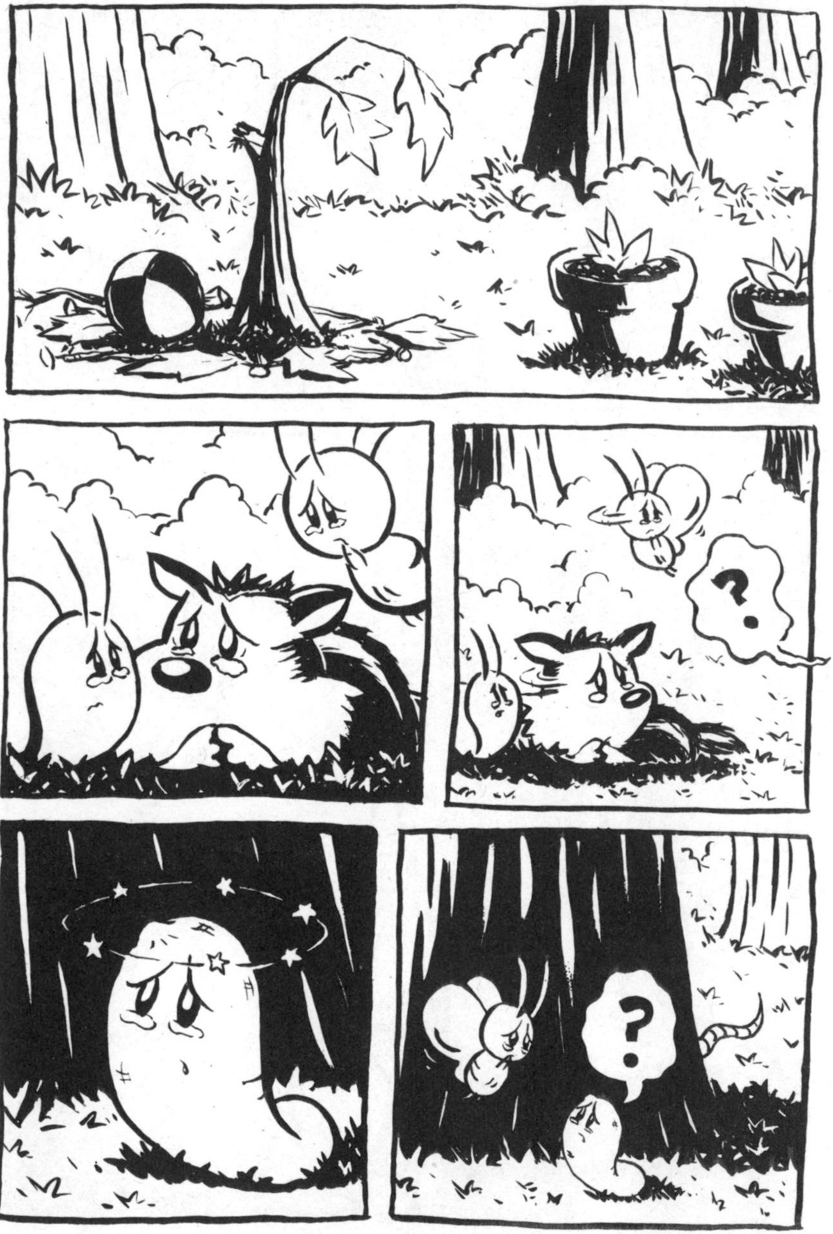
?
?

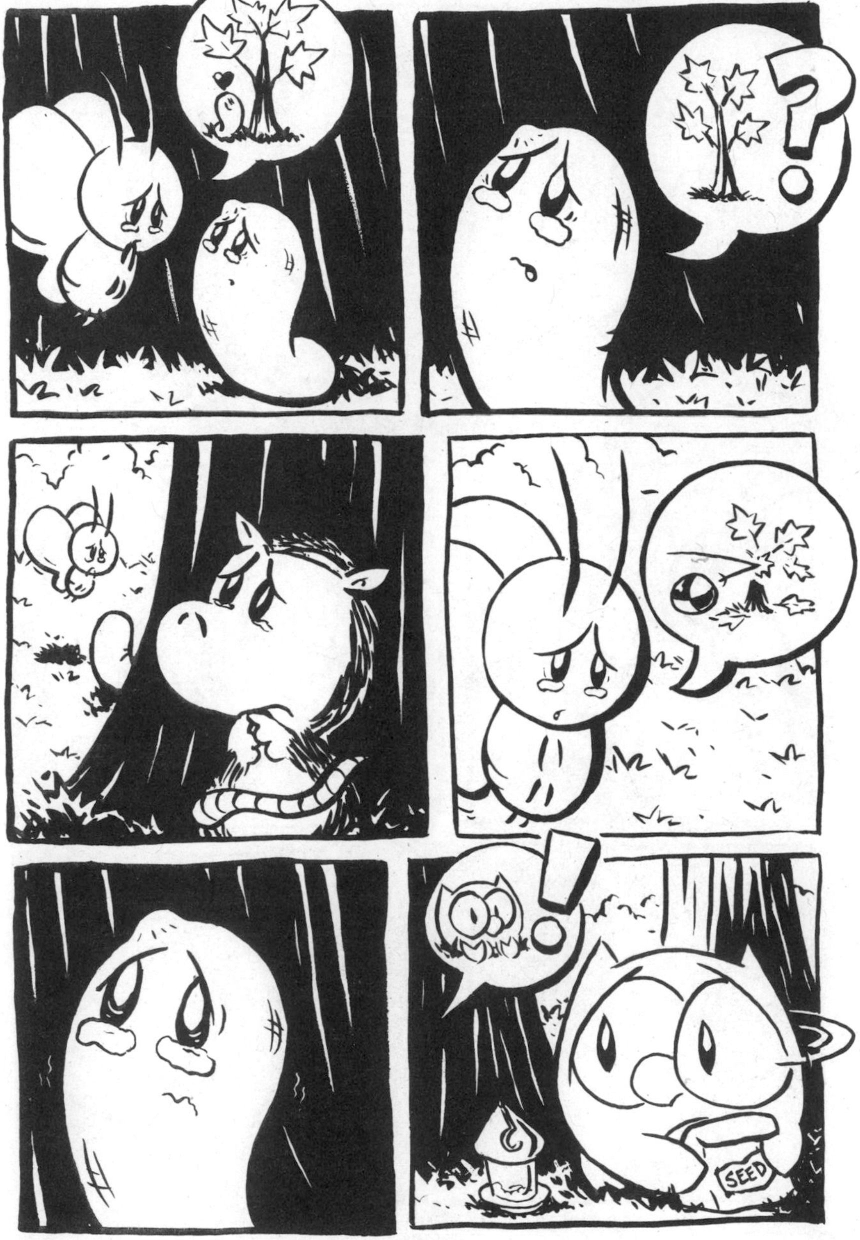
SEED

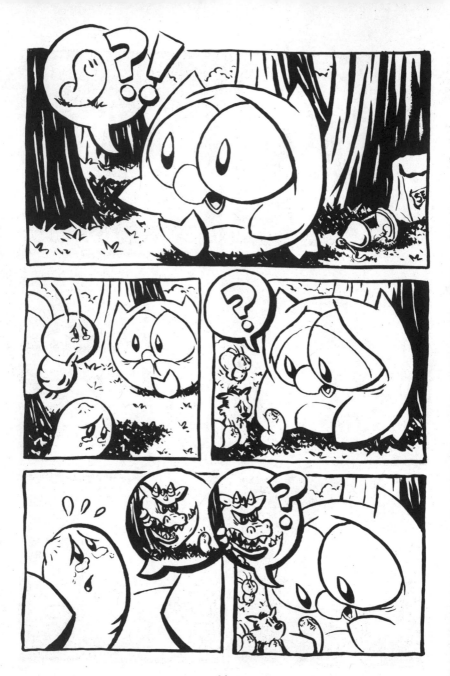

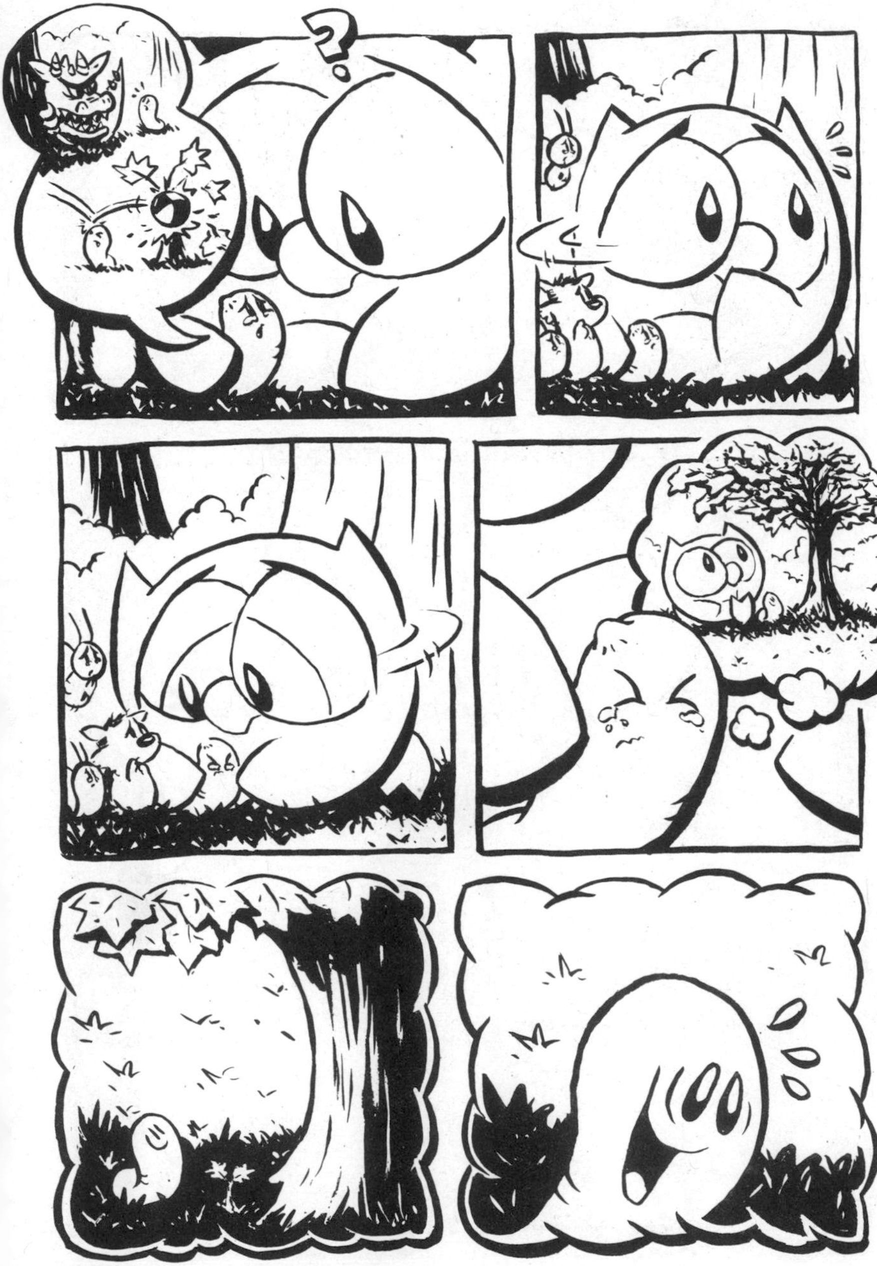
?

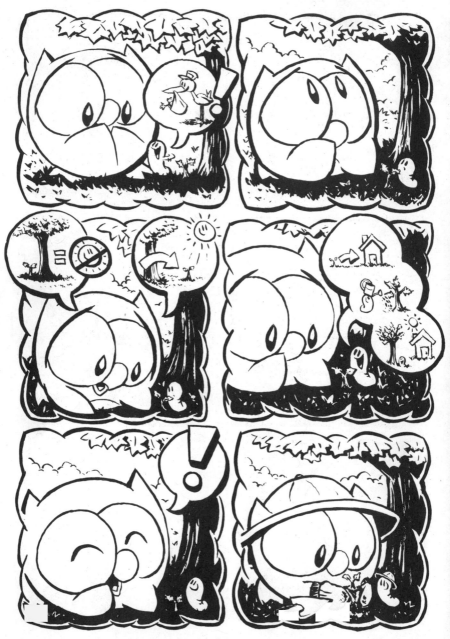

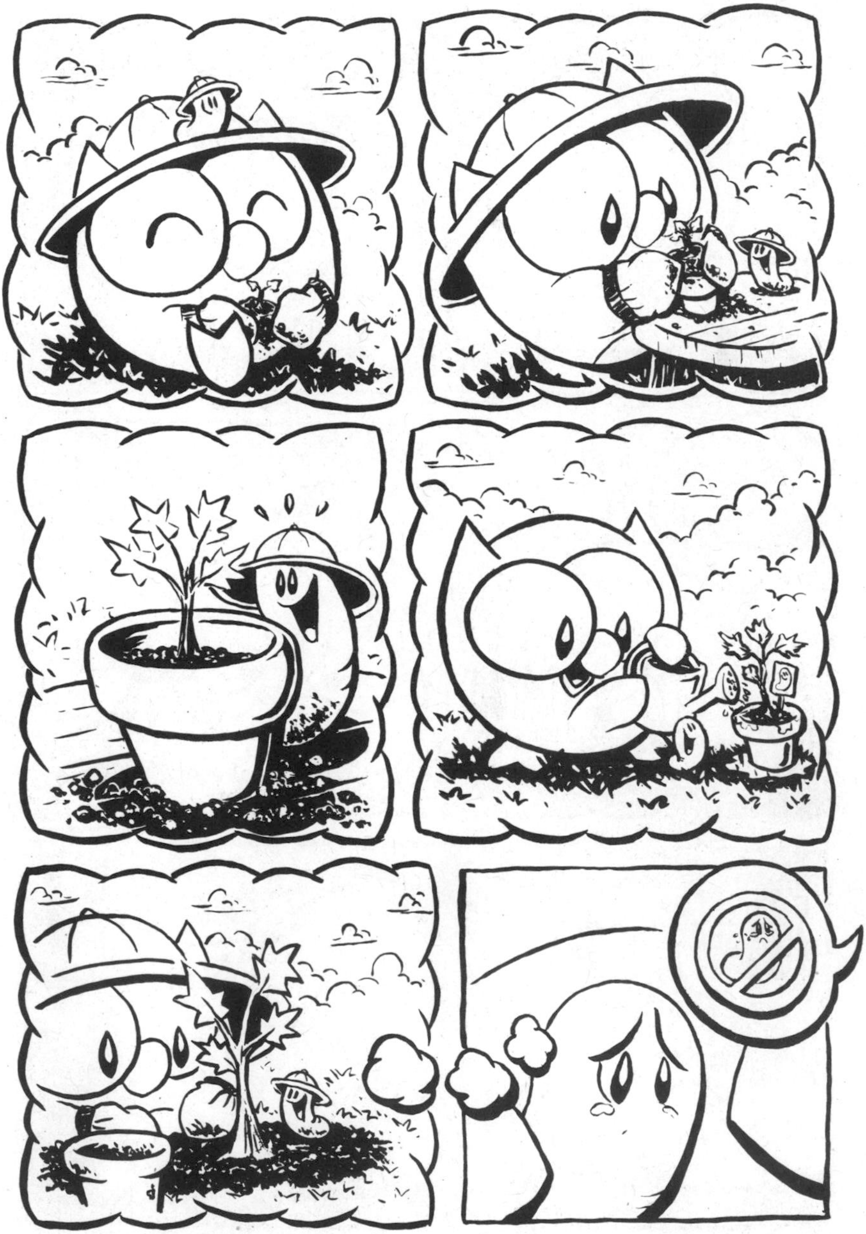

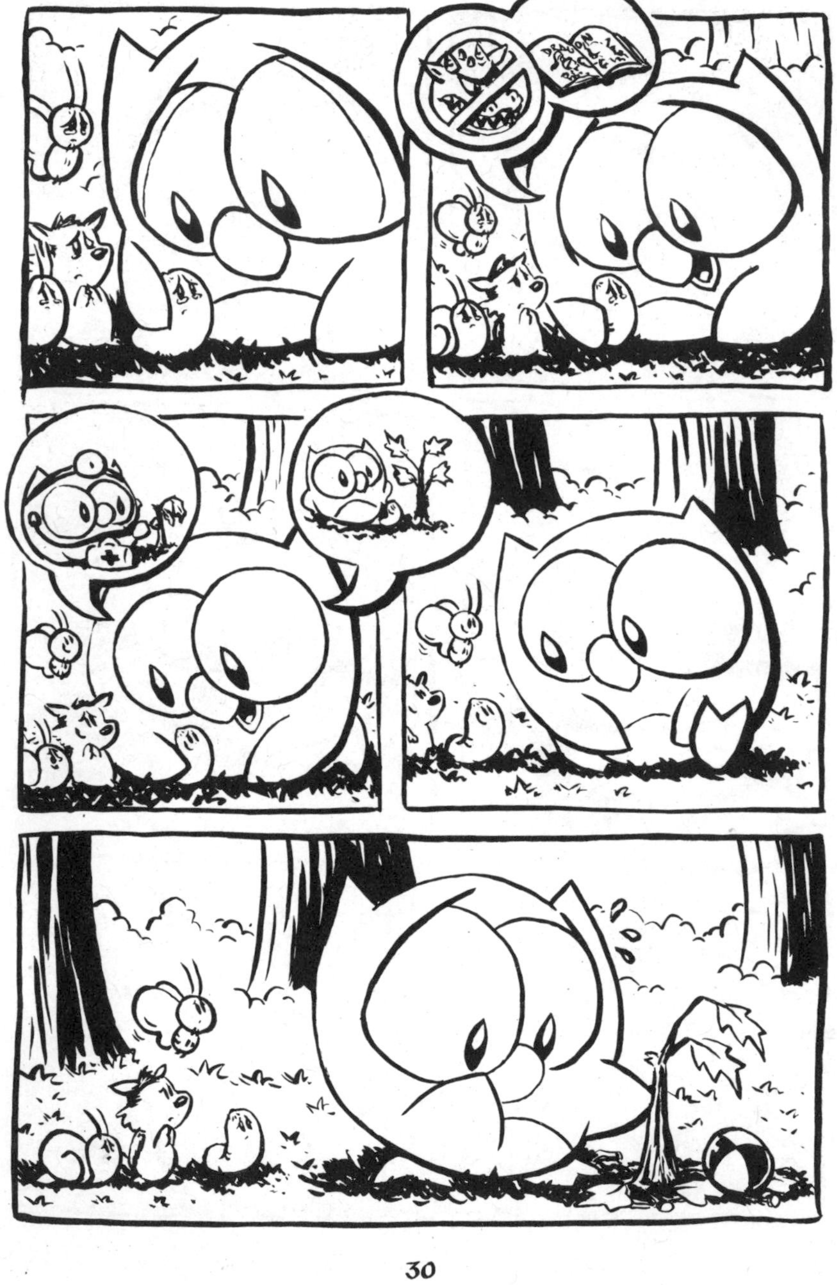
DRAGON

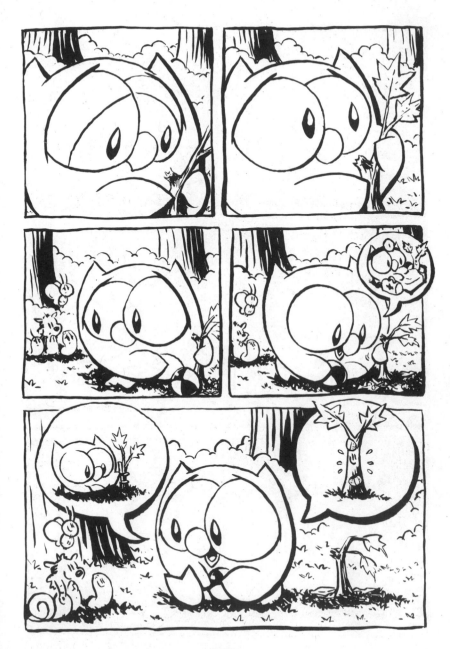

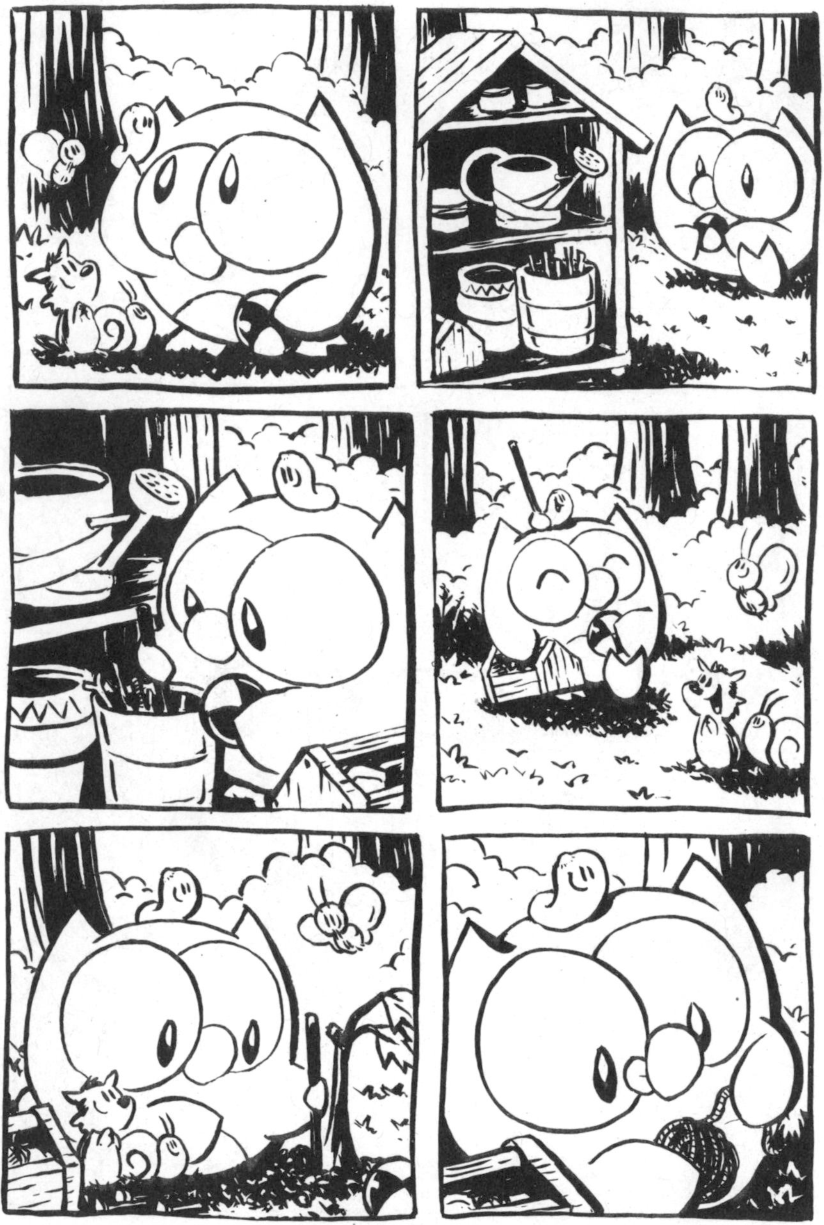

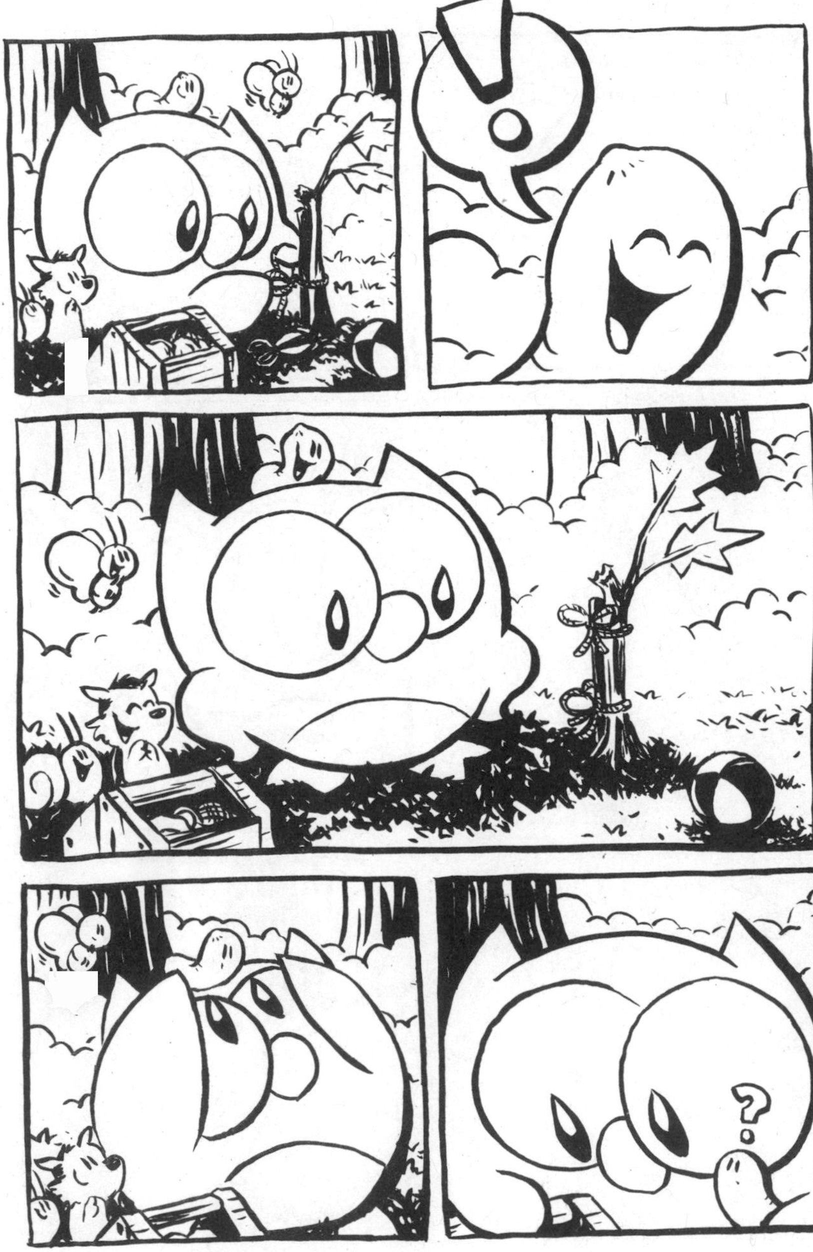
!
?

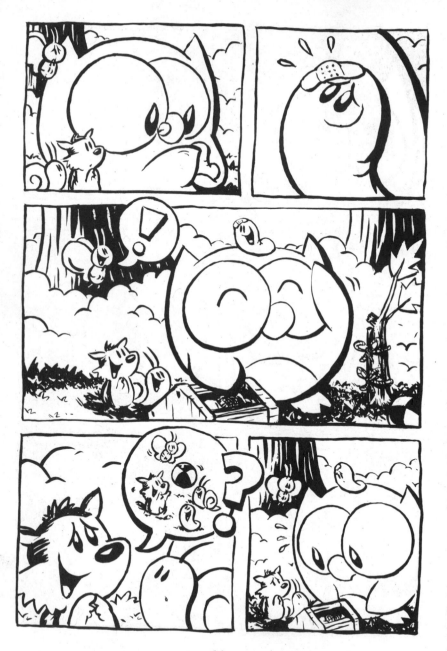

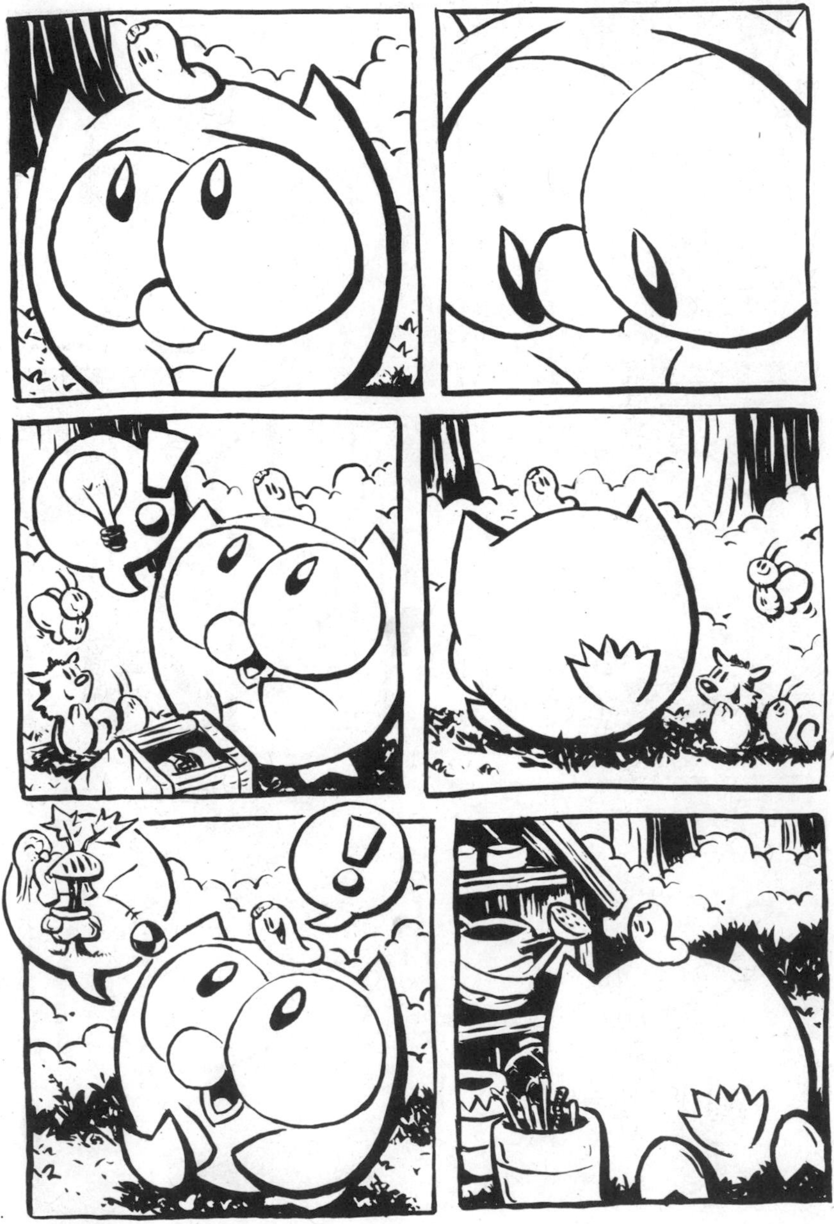
!
!
!

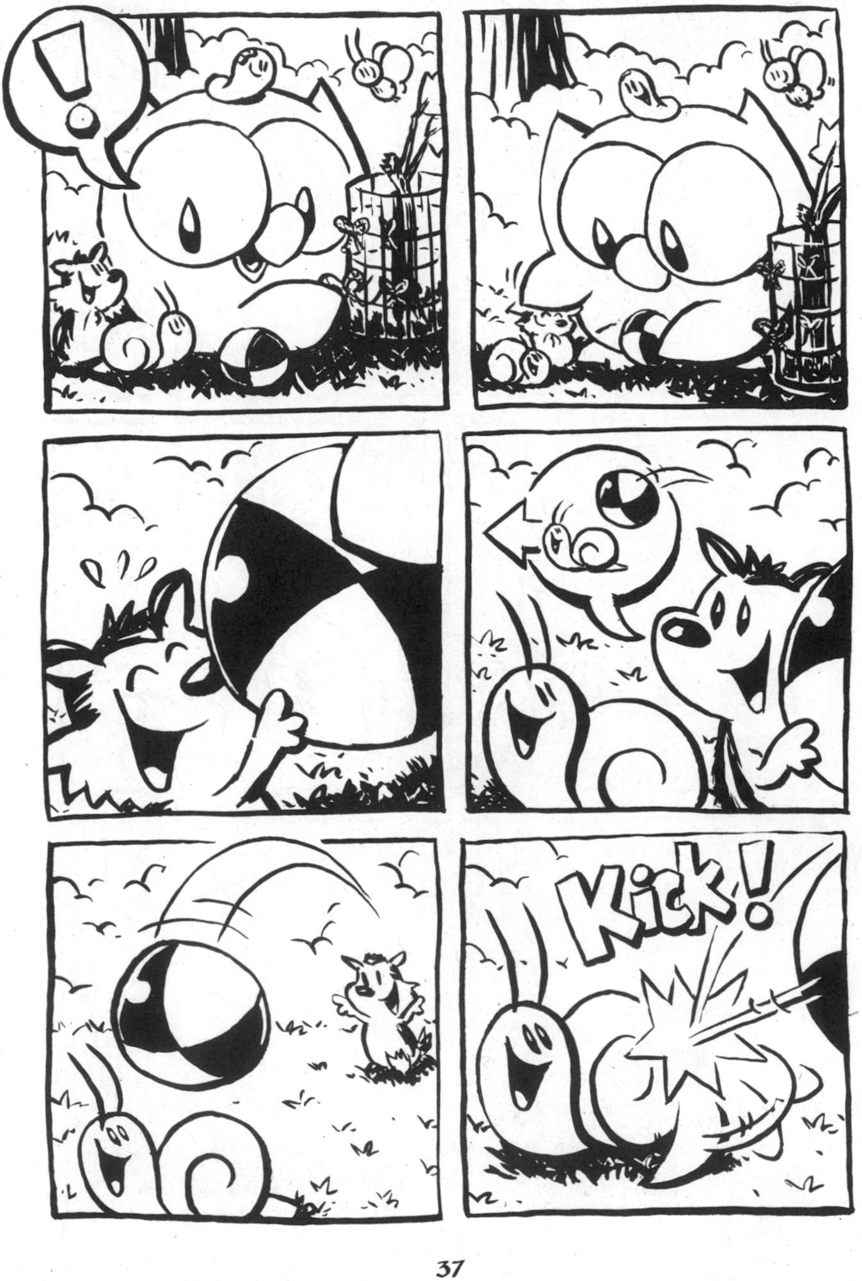
!
Kick!

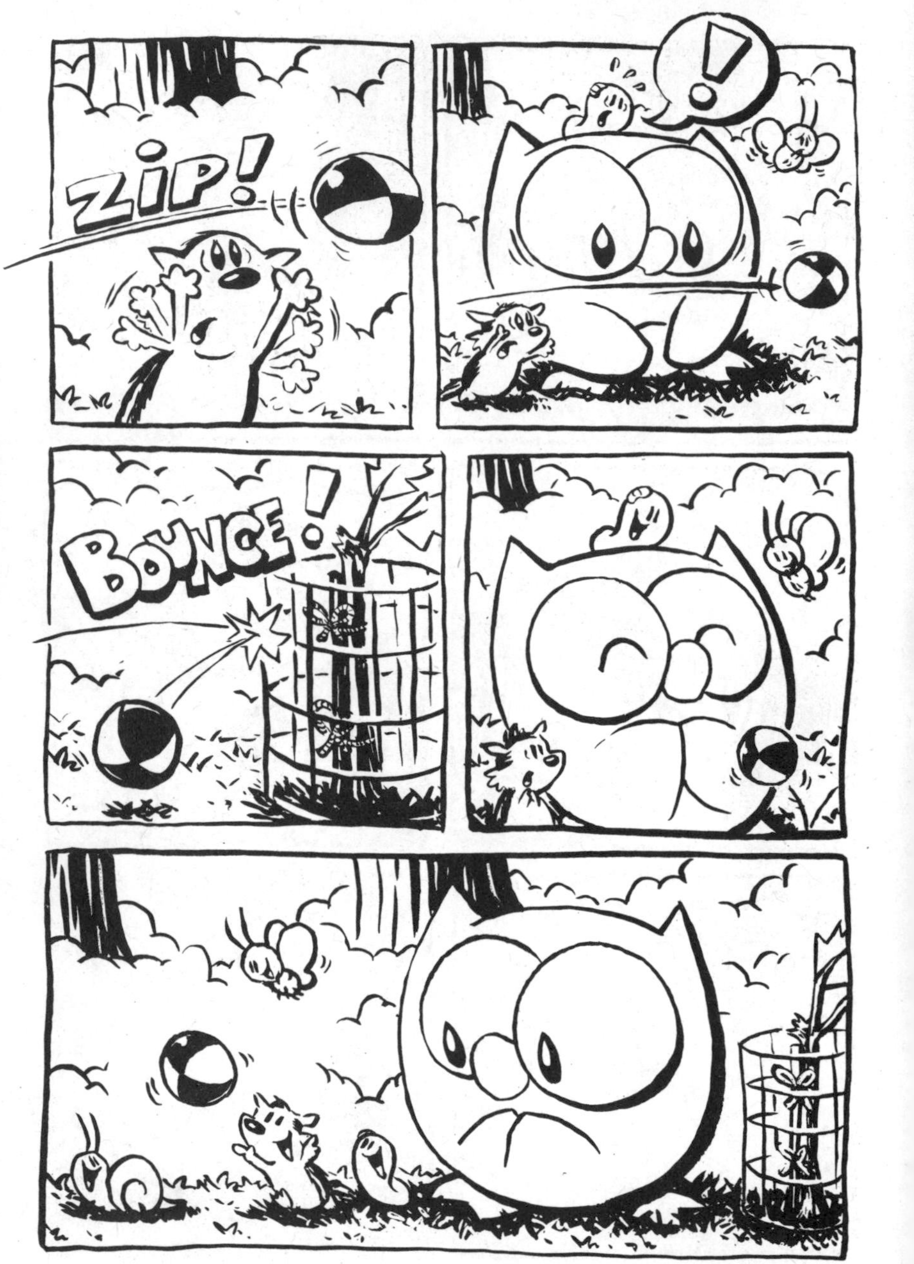
ZIP!
!
BOUNCE!

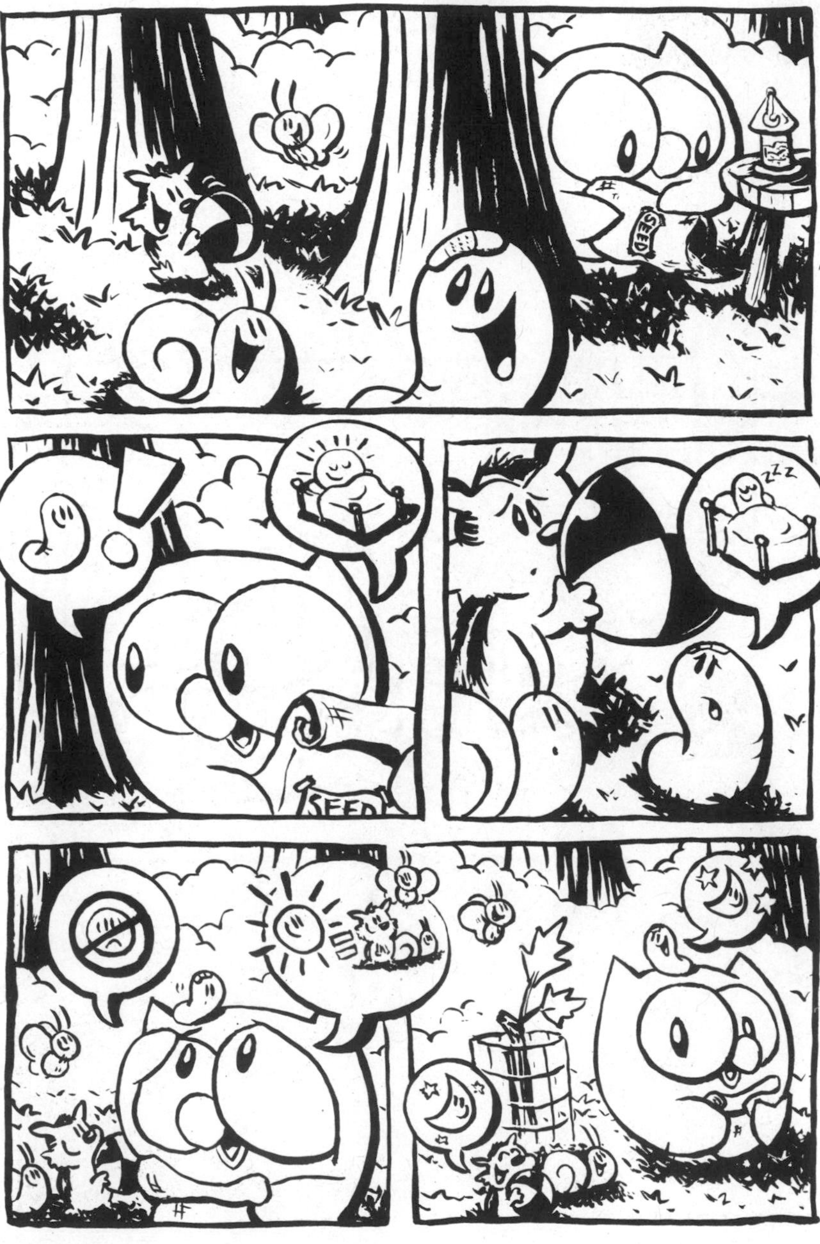
SEED
ZZZ
SEED

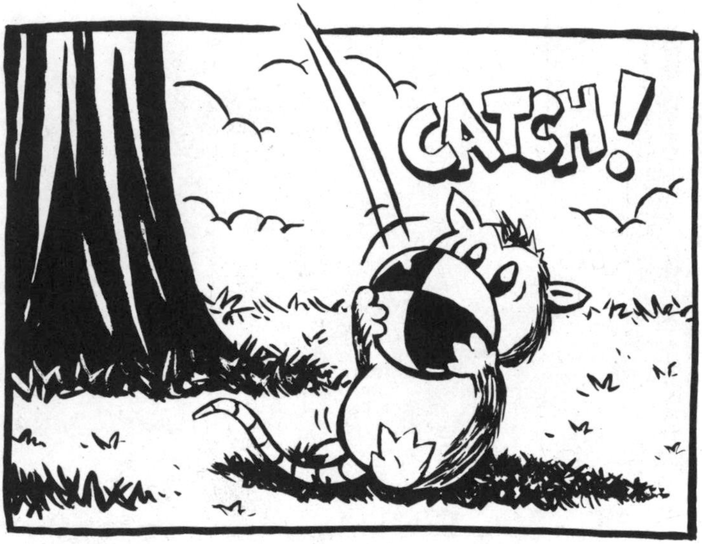
CATCH!

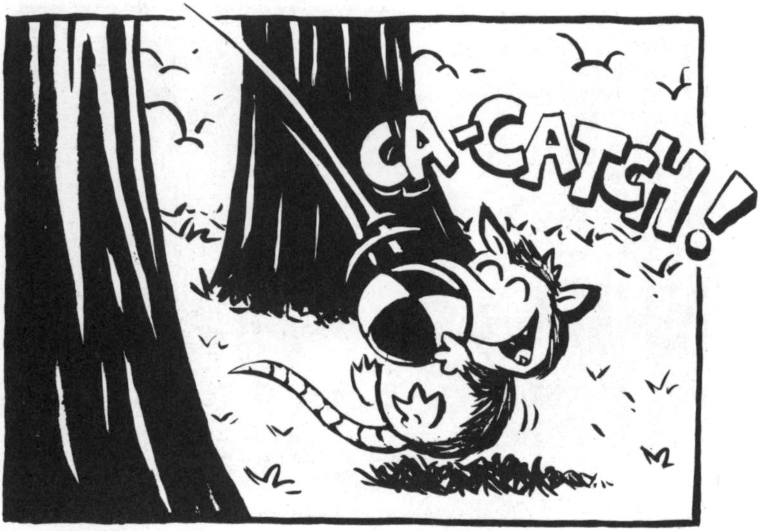
CA-CATCH!

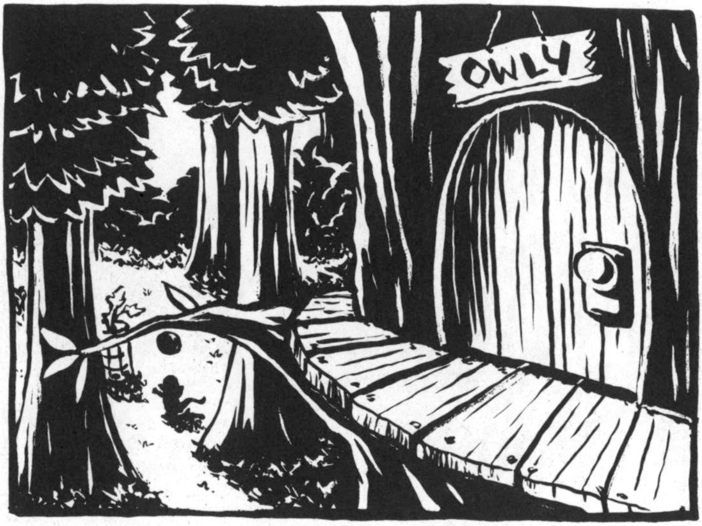
OWLY

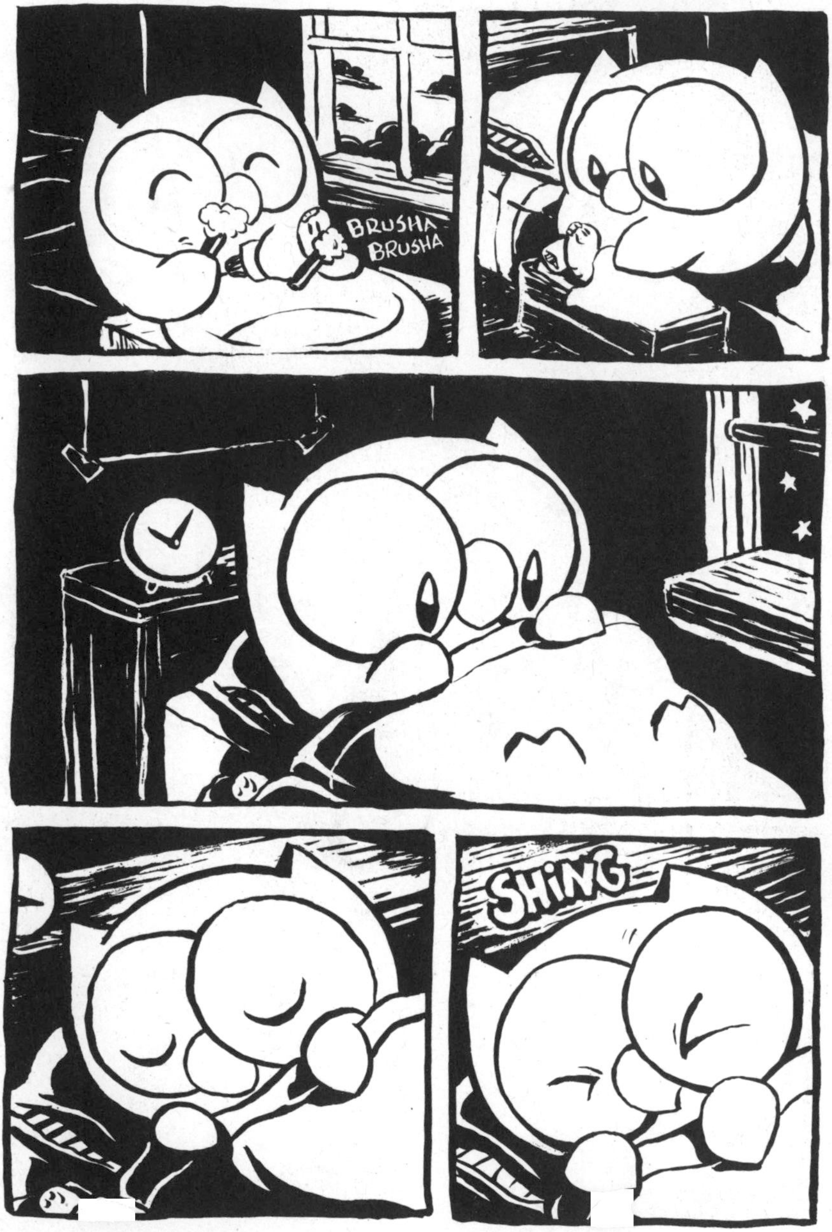
BRUSHA
BRUSHA
SHING

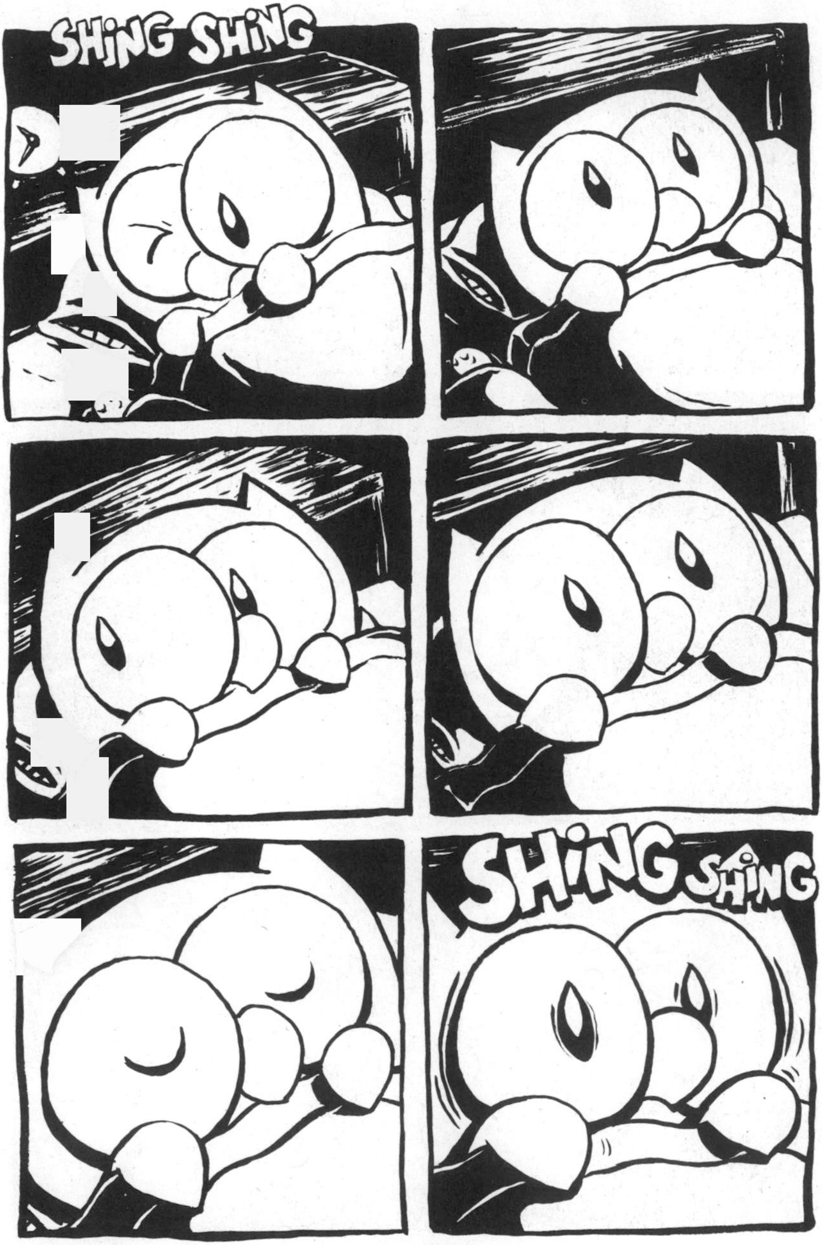
SHING SHING
SHING SHING

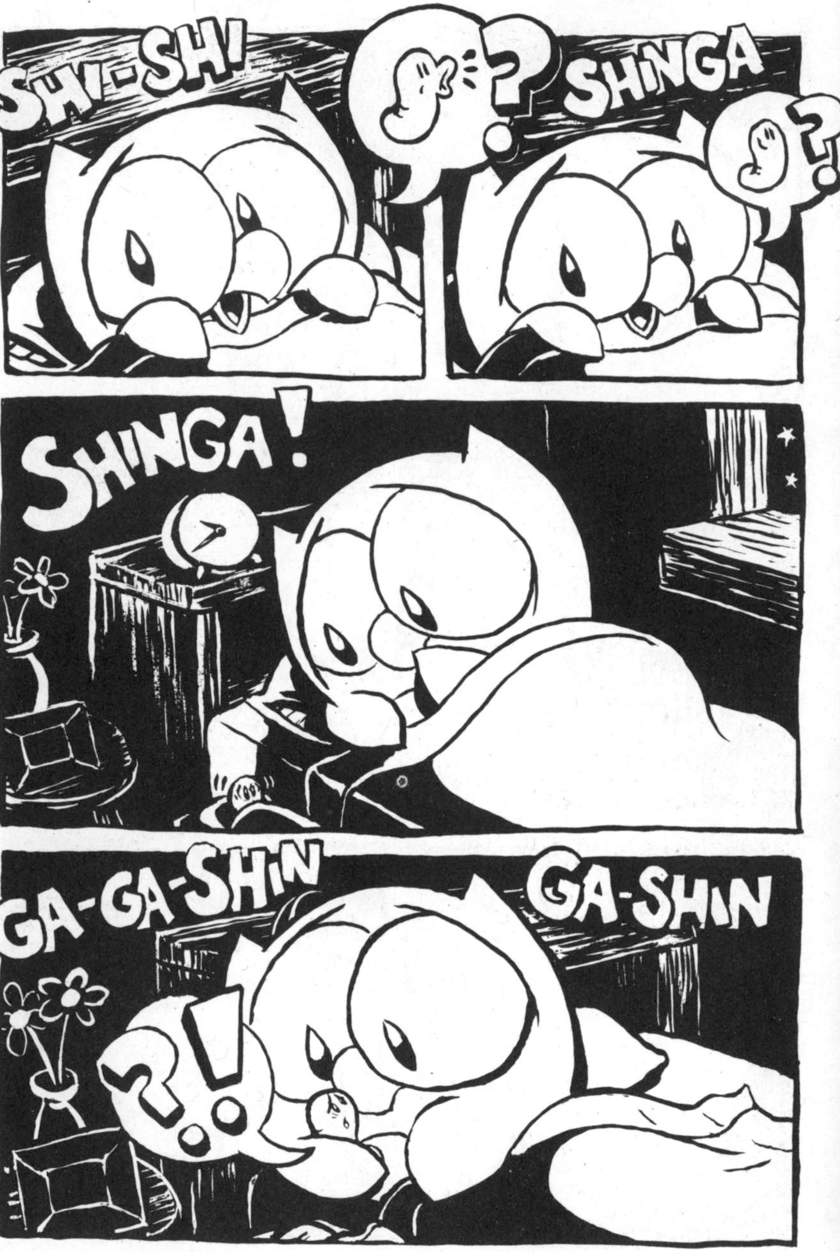
SHI-SHI
?
SHINGA
?
SHINGA!
GA-GA-SHIN
GA-SHIN
?!

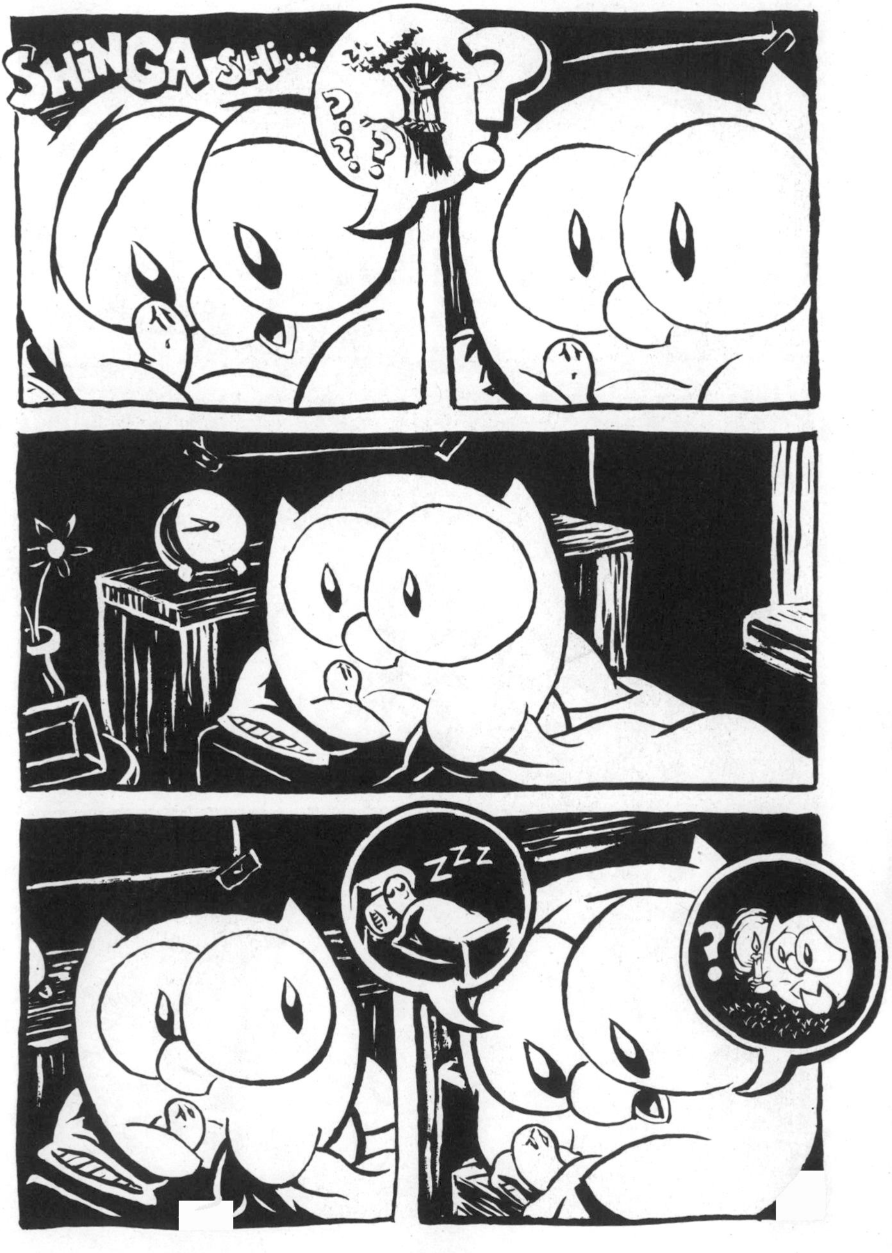
SHiNGA SHi...
?
?
Z Z Z
?

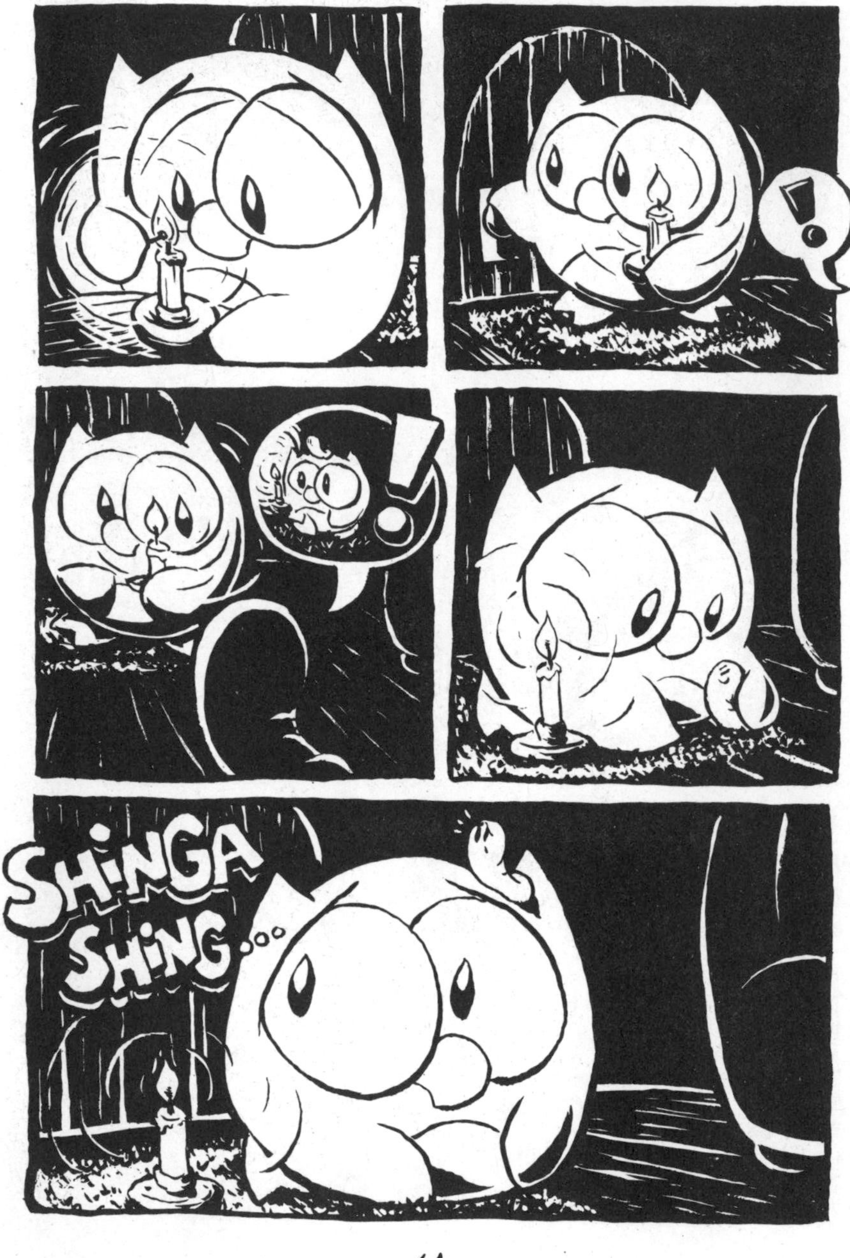
!
!
SHINGA SHING...

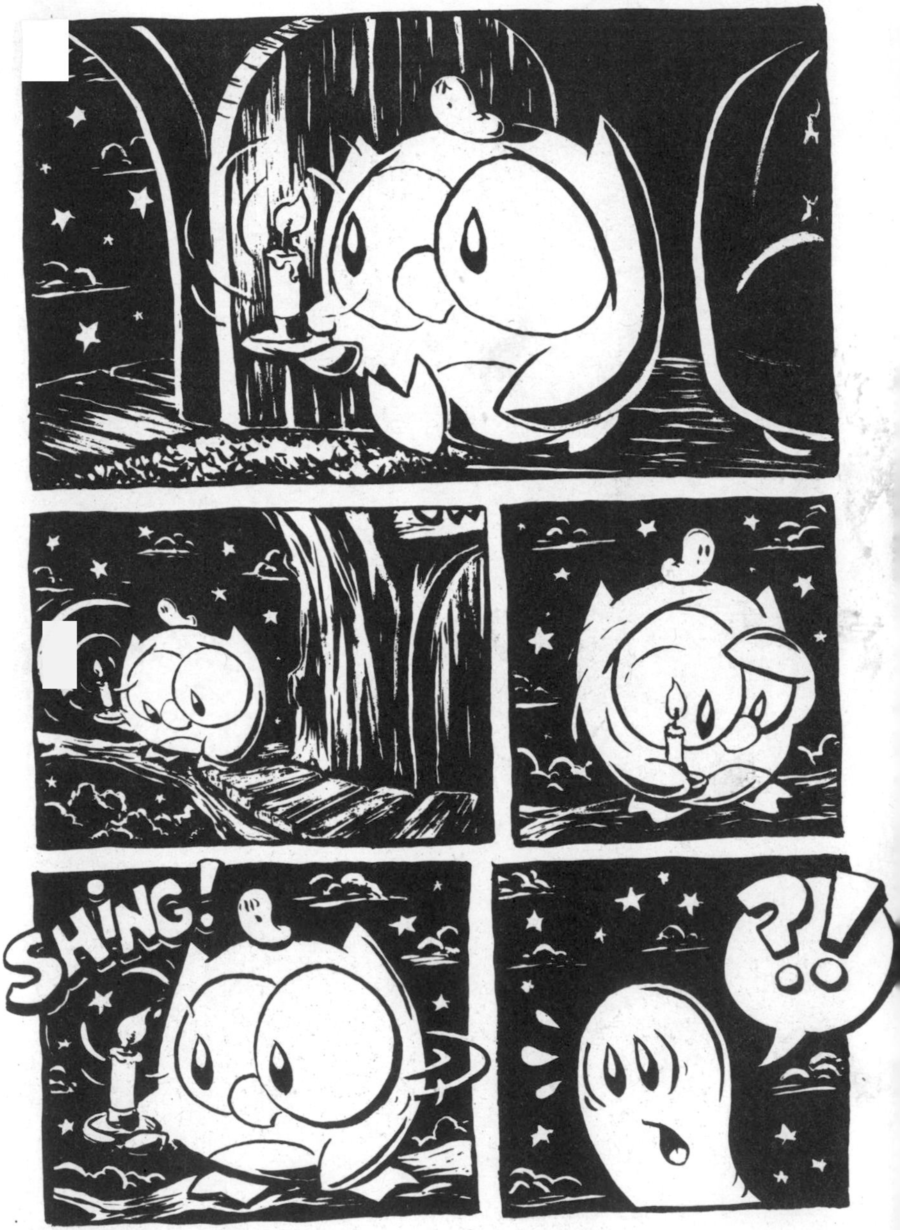
SHING!
?!

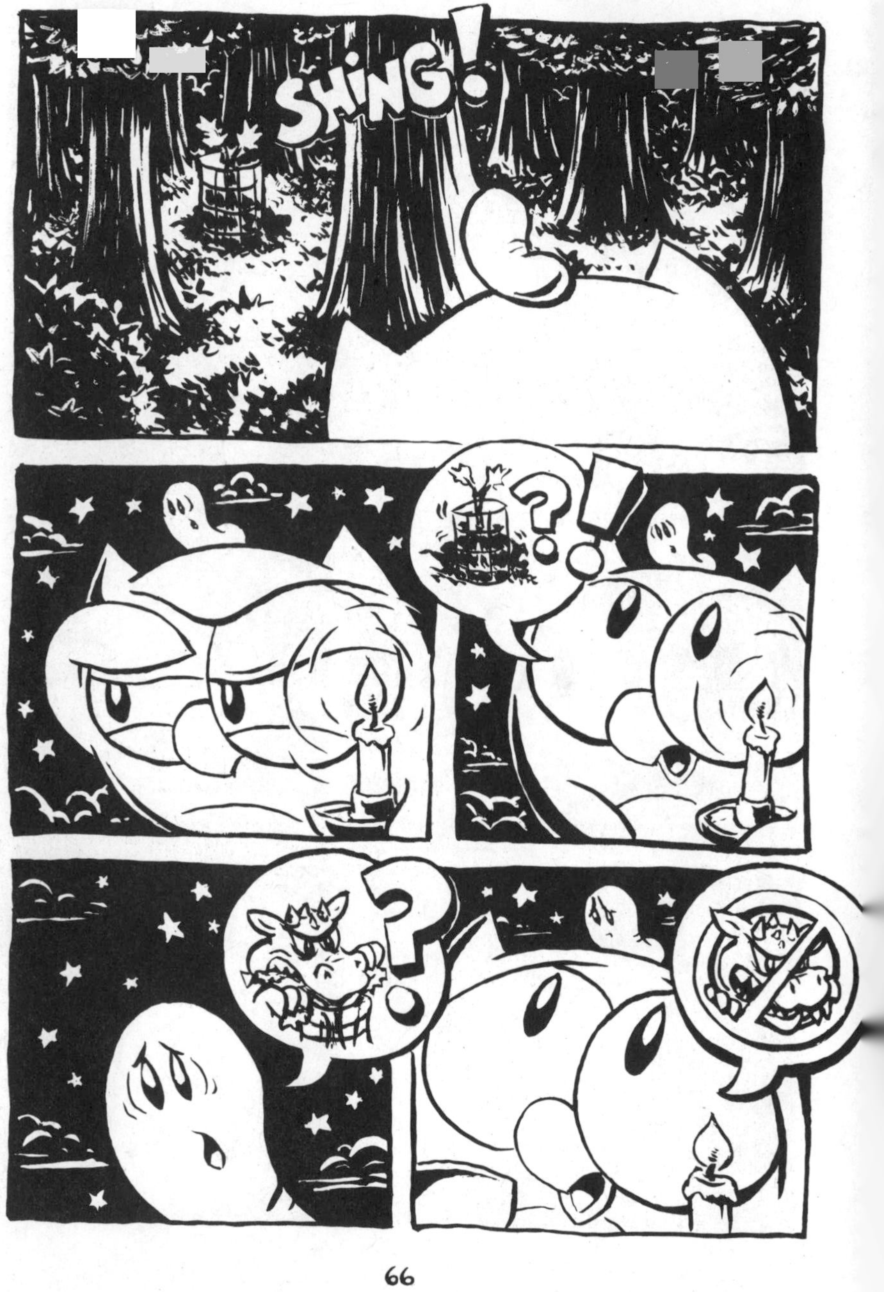
SHING!
?!
?

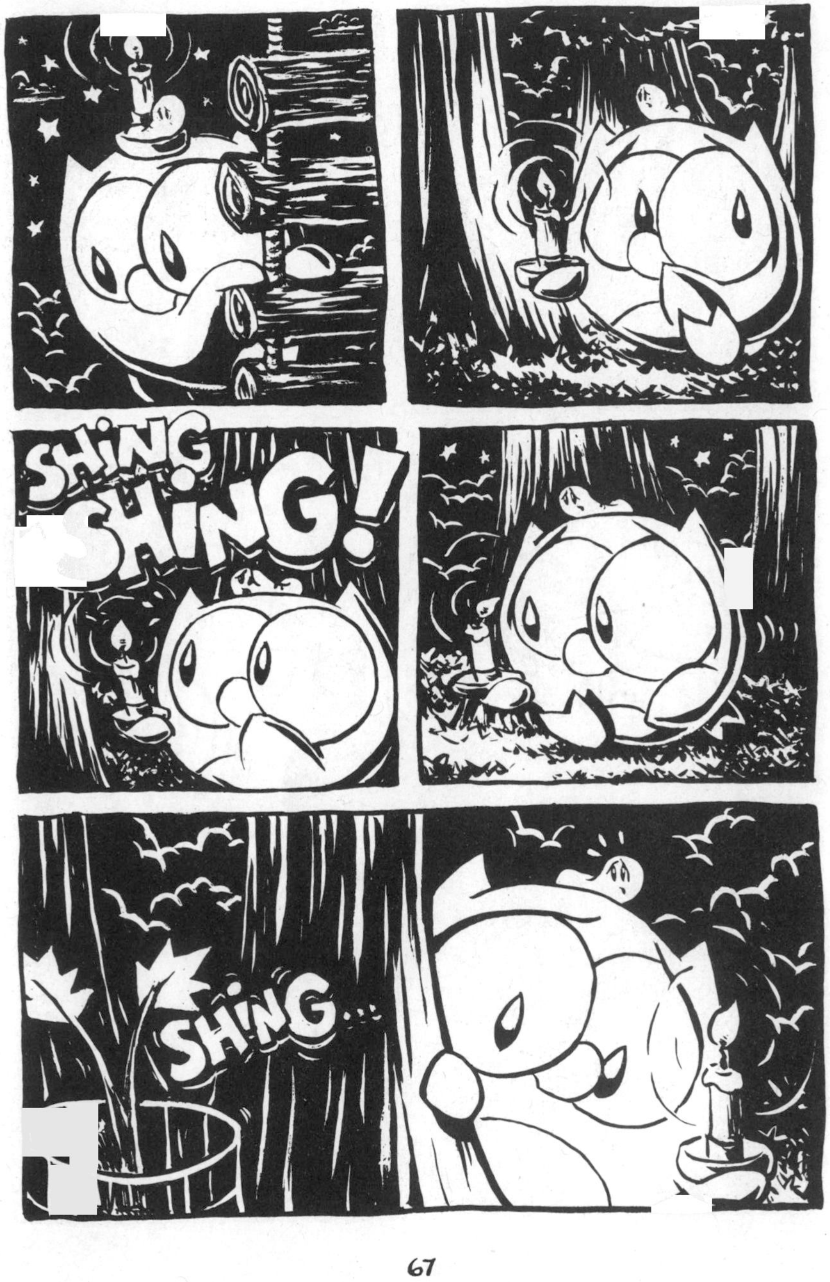
SHING
SHING!
SHING...

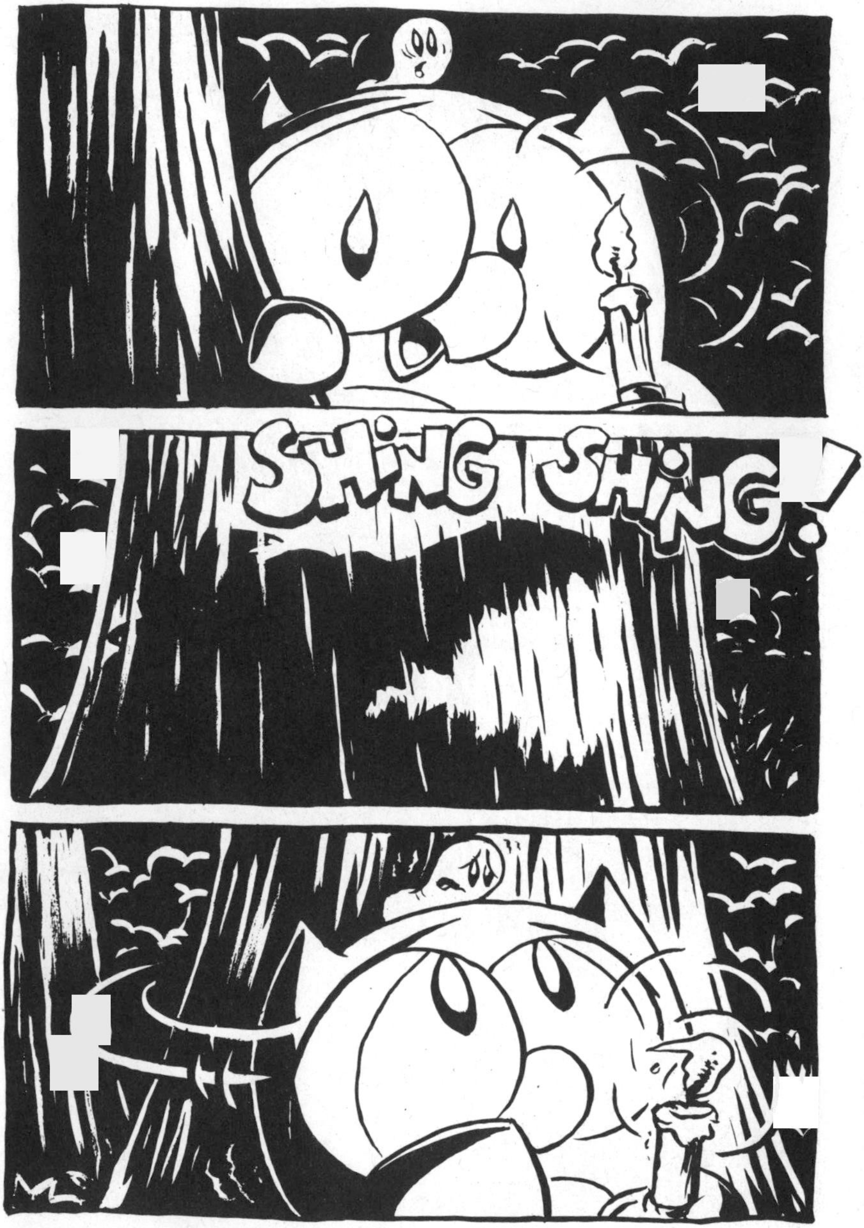
SHING SHING!

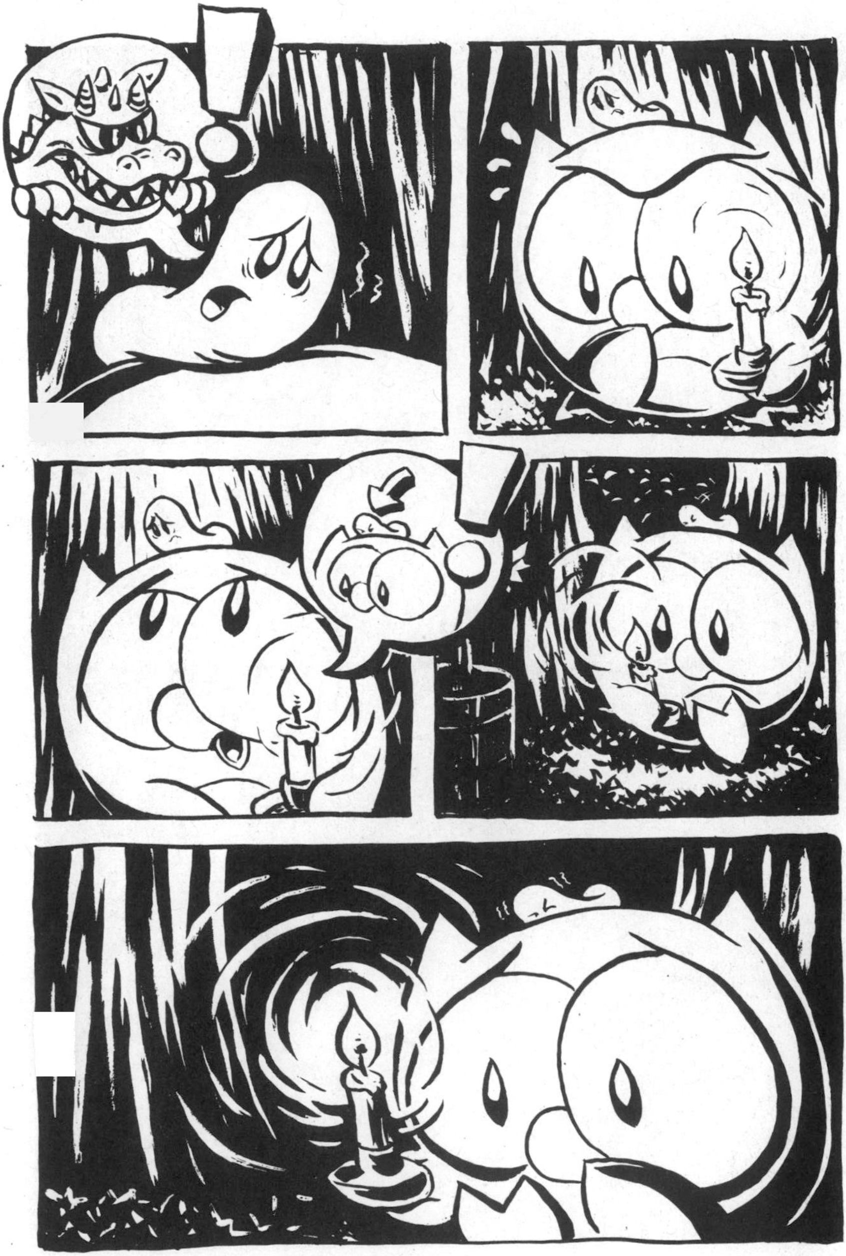

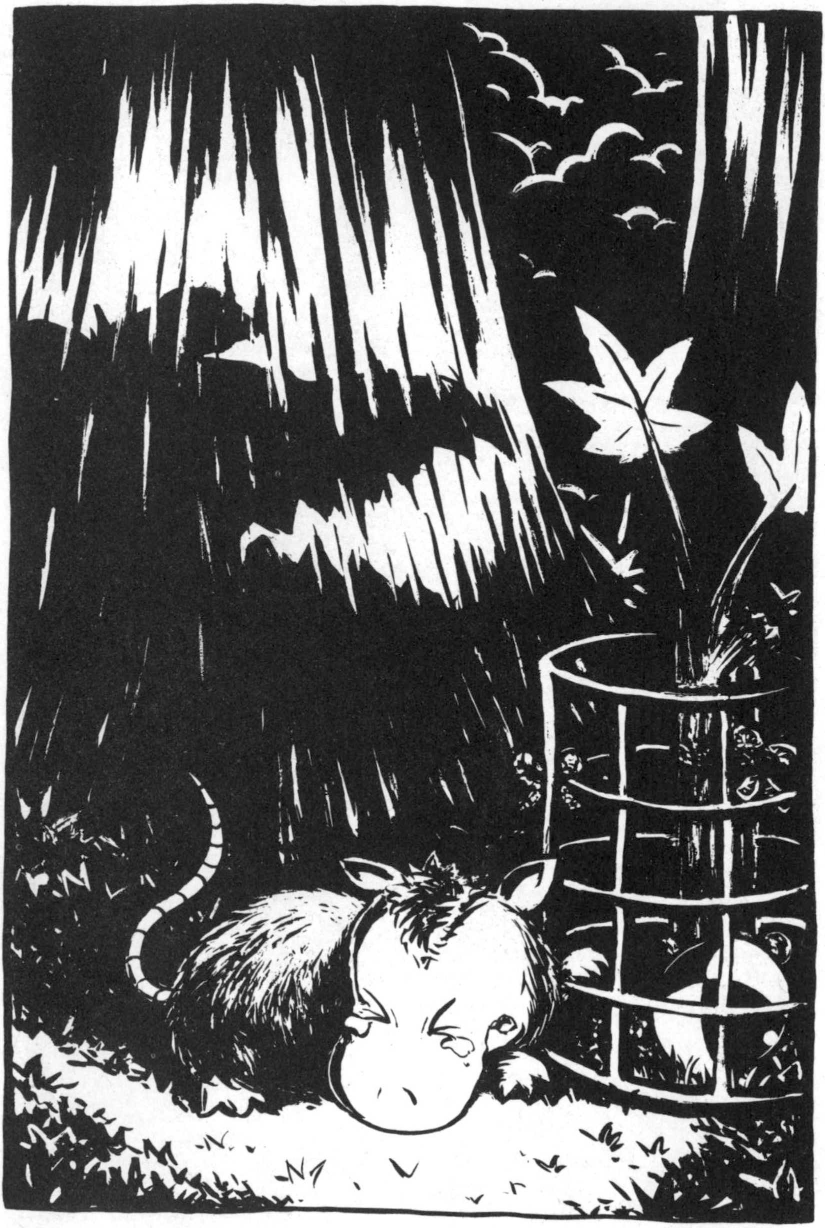

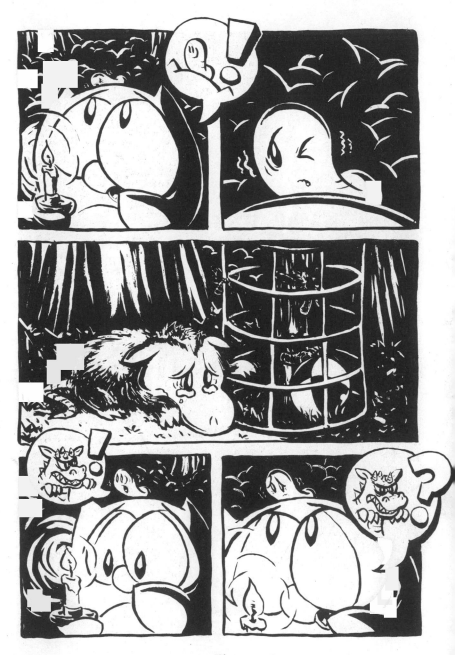

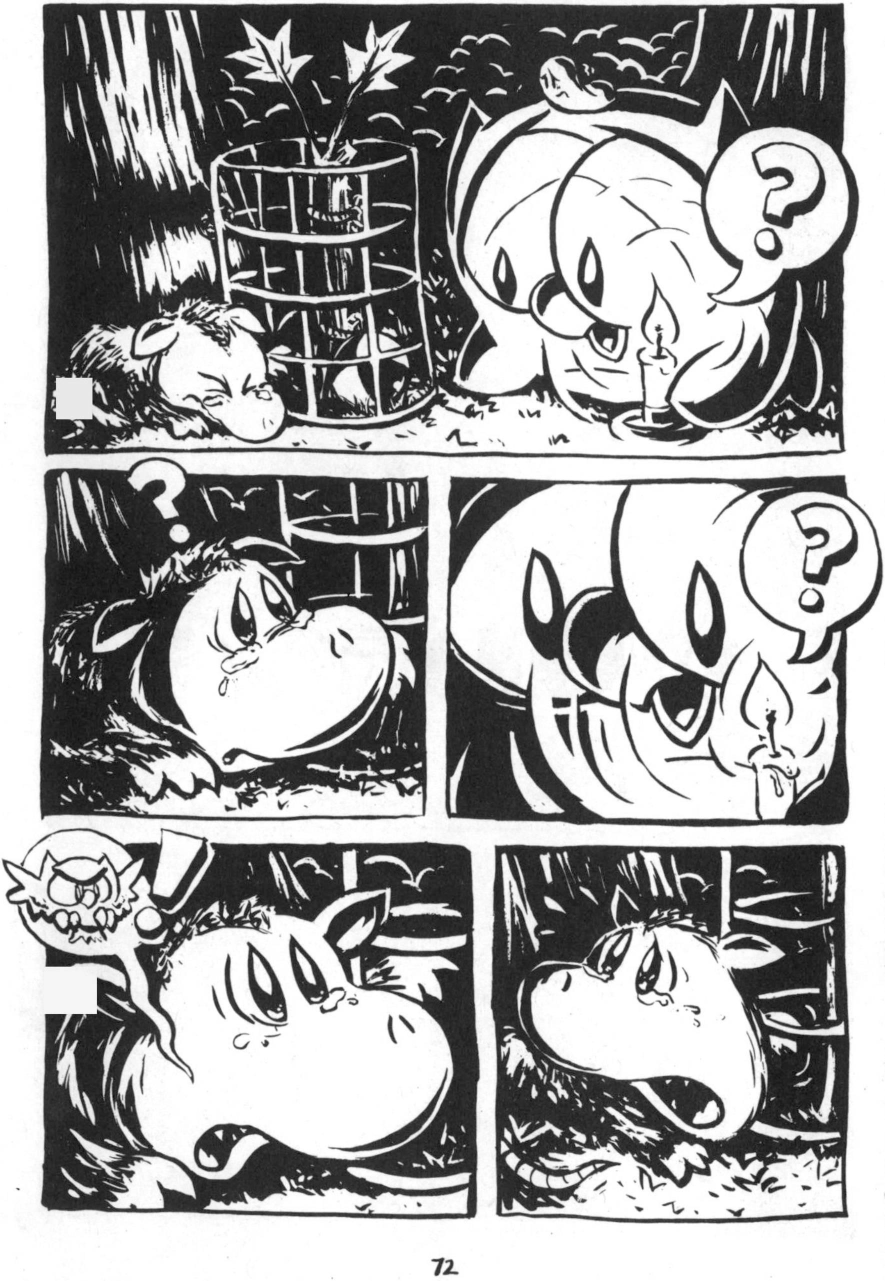
?
?
?
!

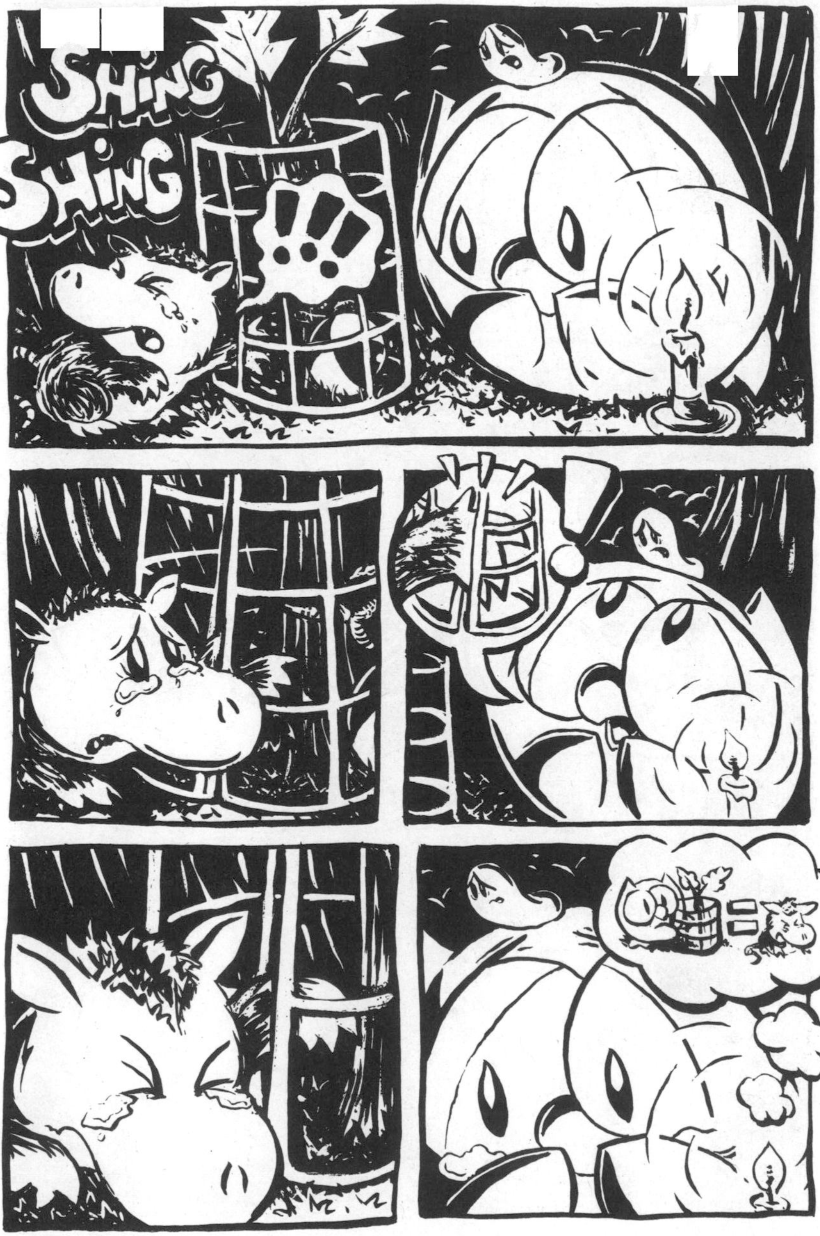
SHING
SHING
!!
!

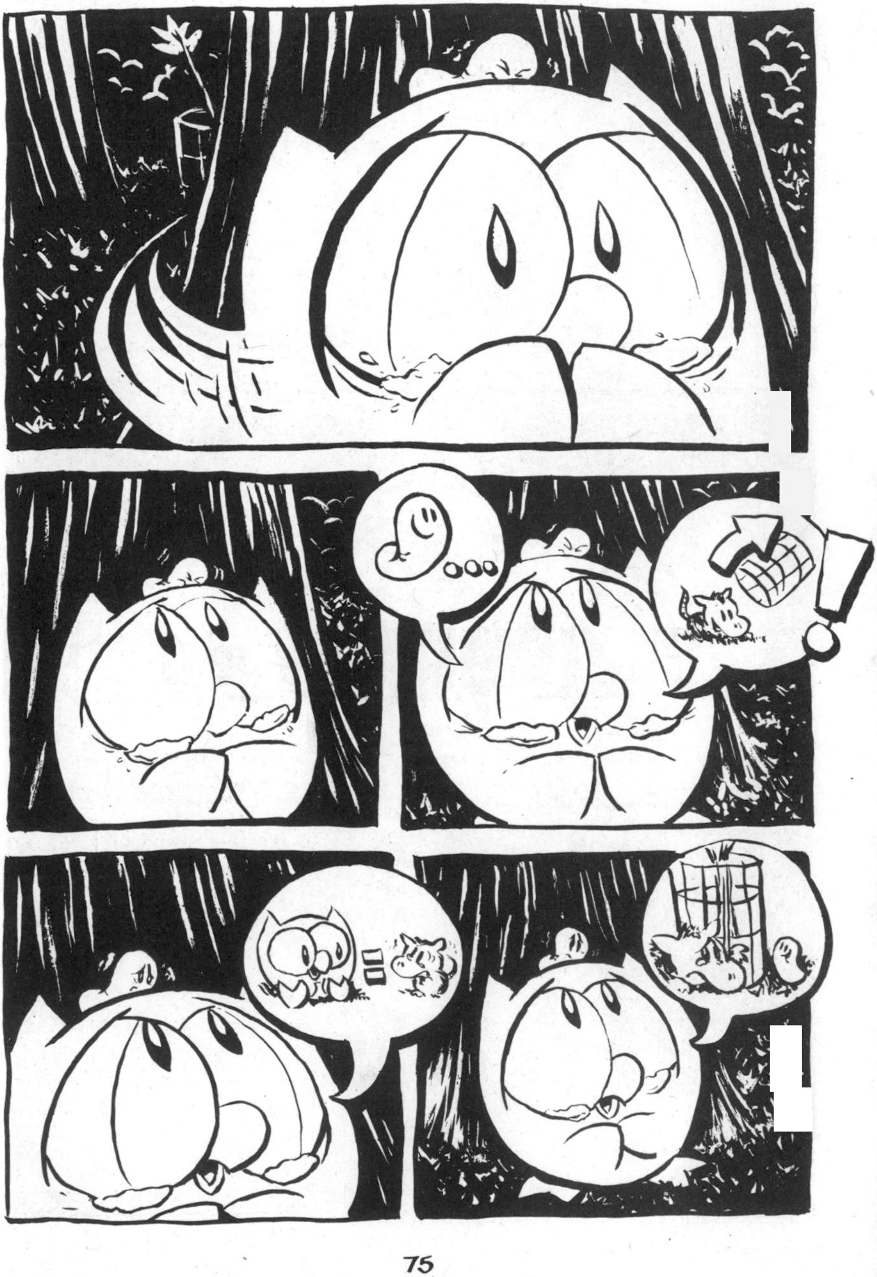

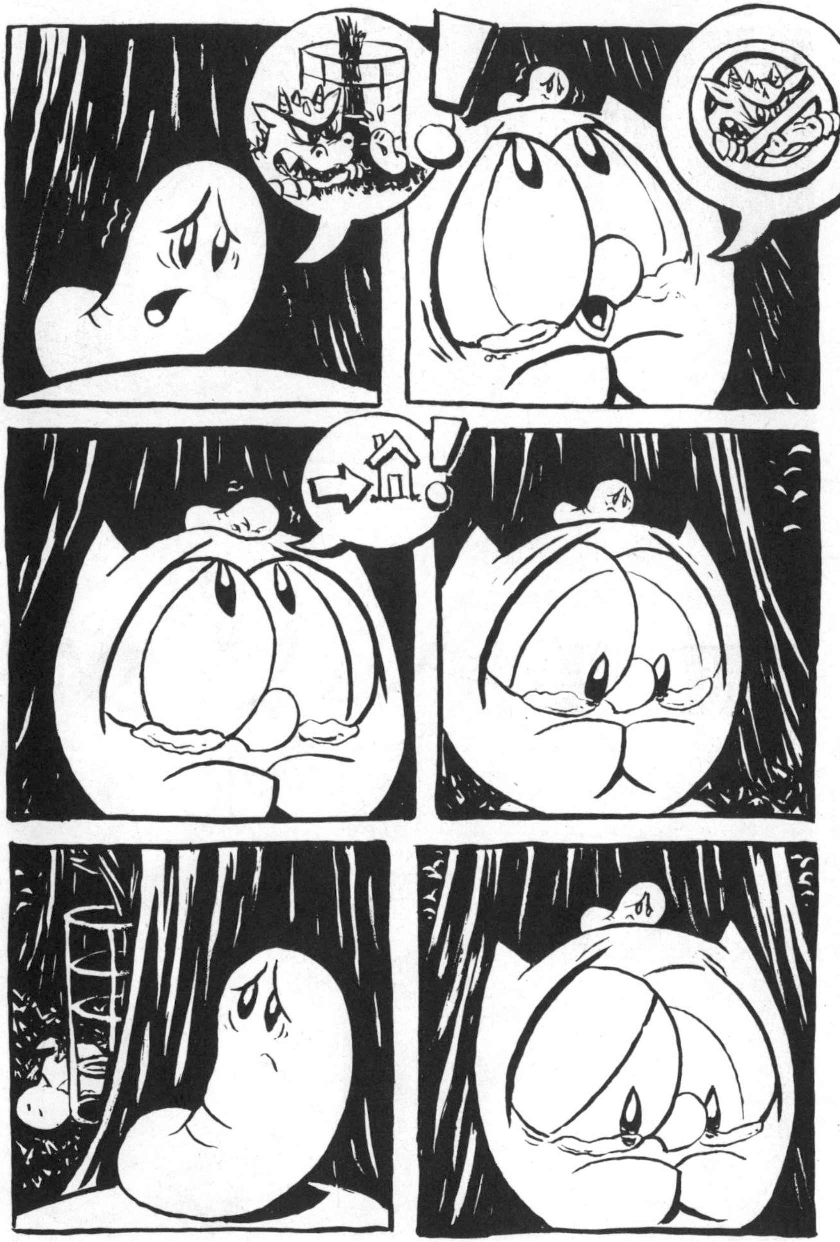

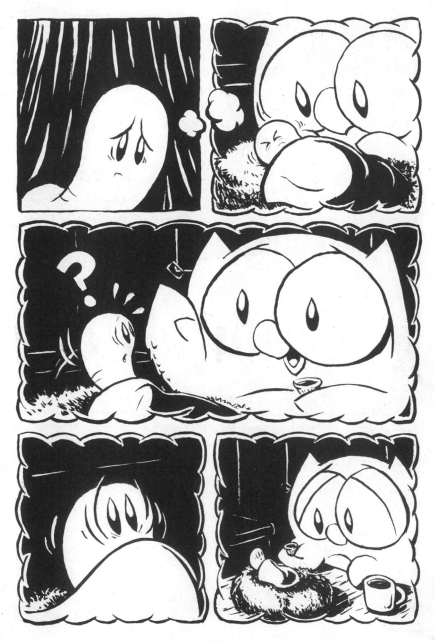

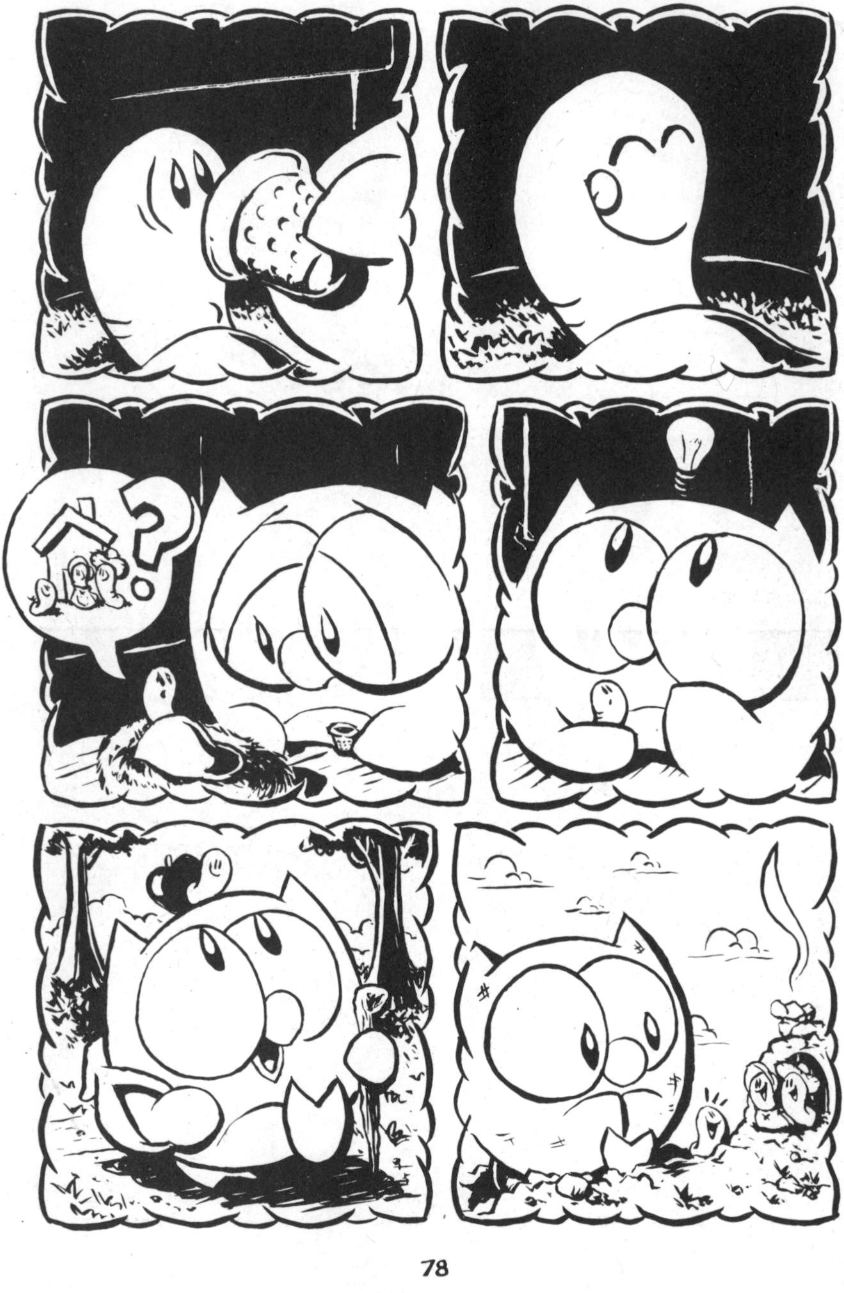

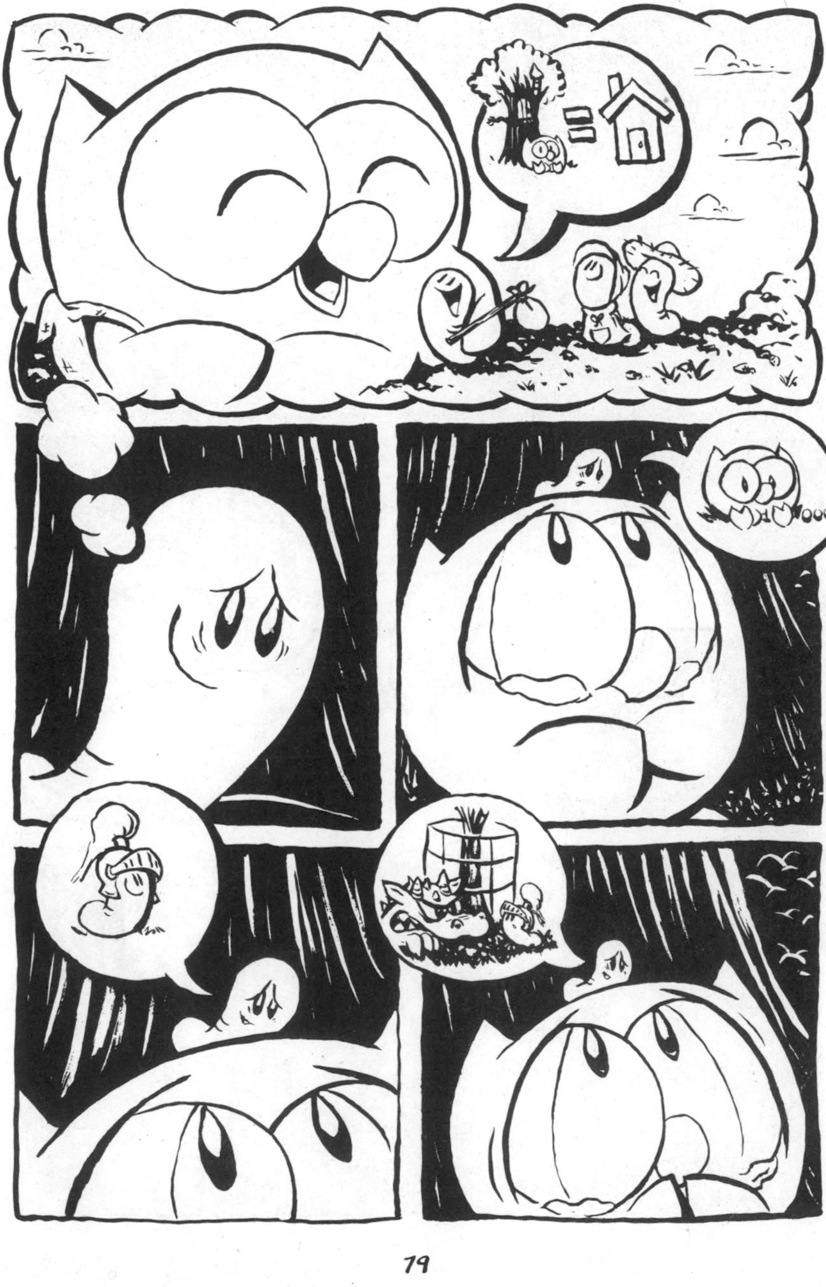

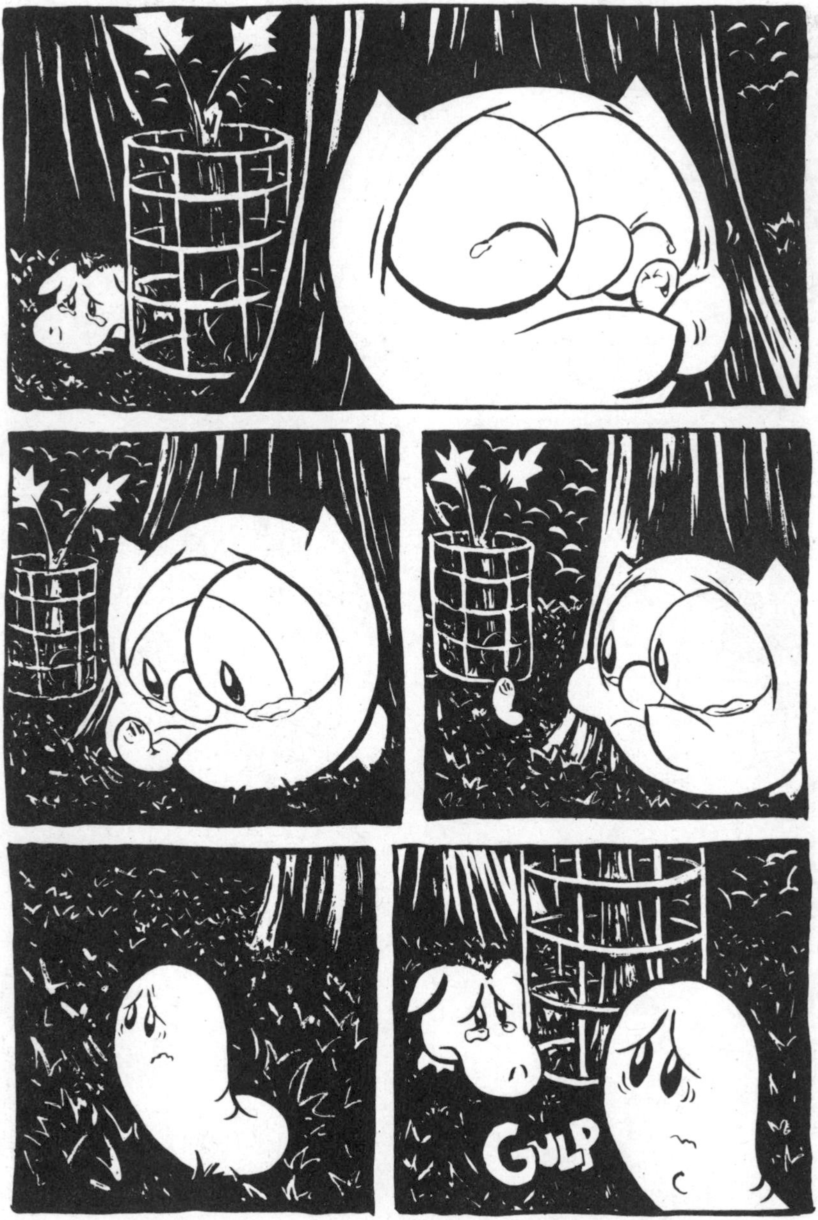
GULP

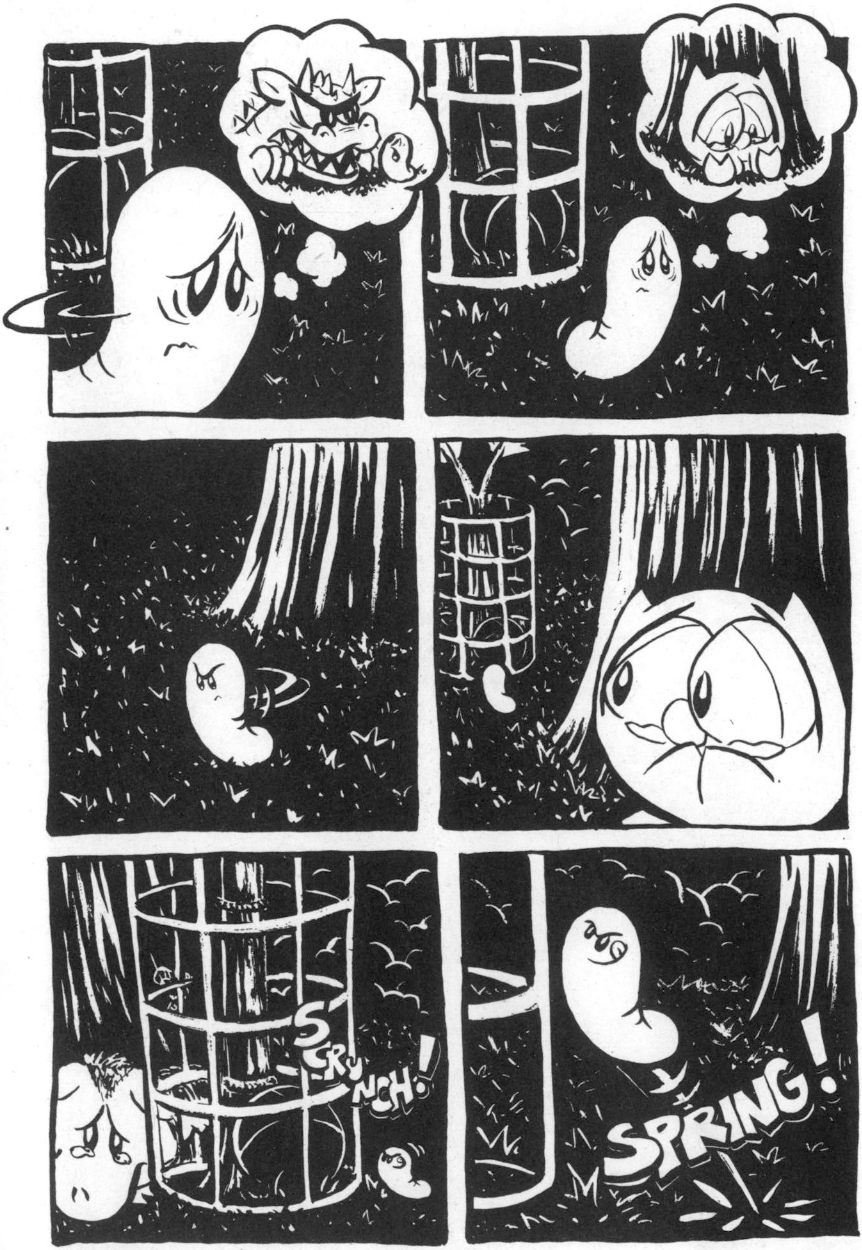
SCRUNCH!
SPRING!

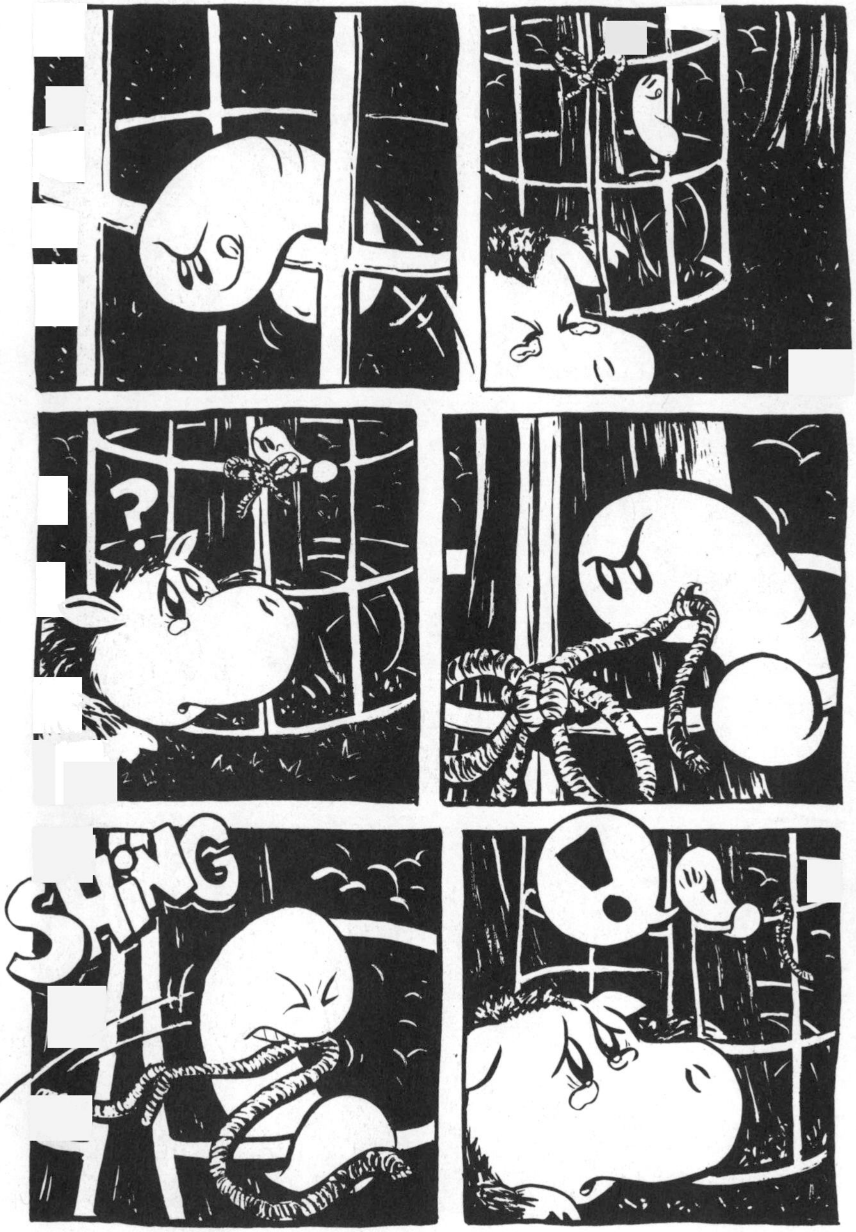
?
SHING
!

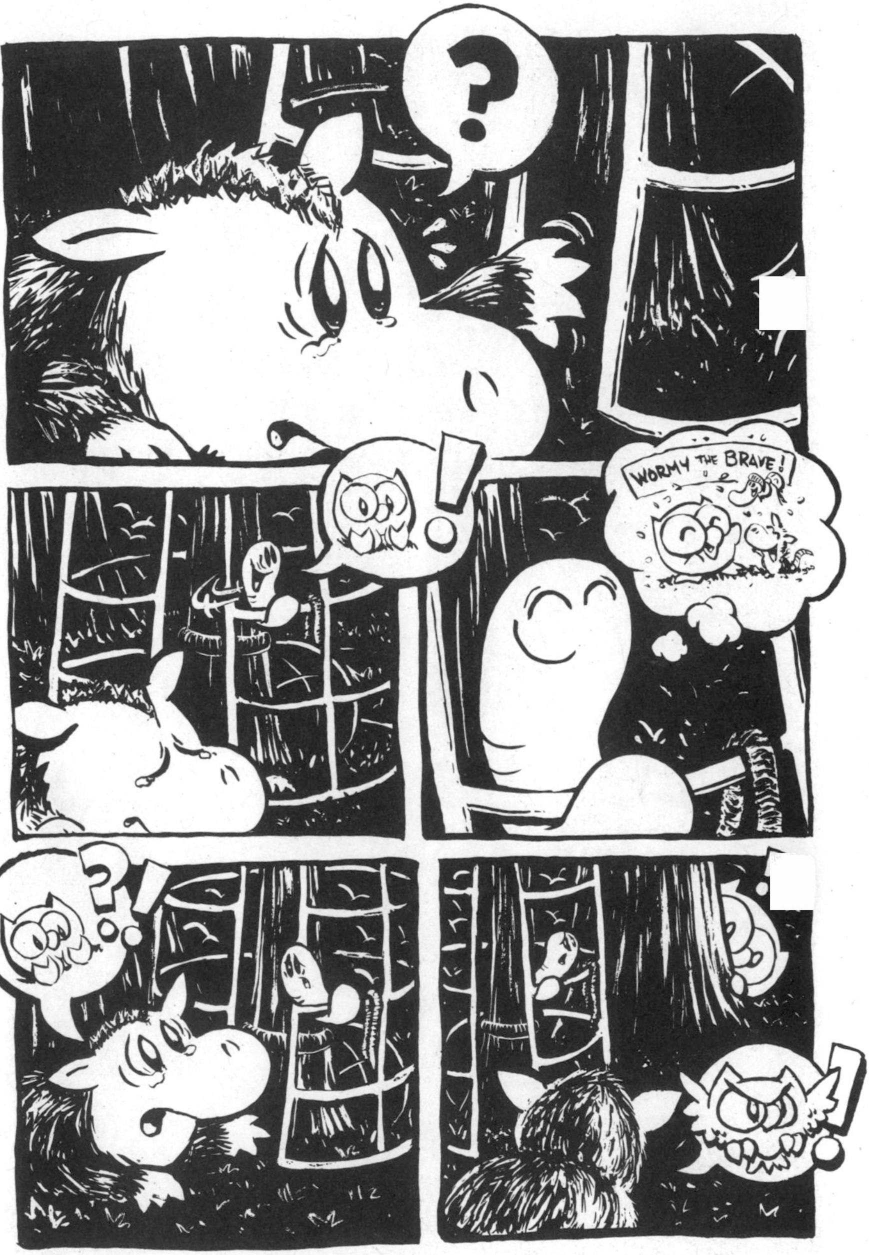
?
!
WORMY THE BRAVE!
?!
!

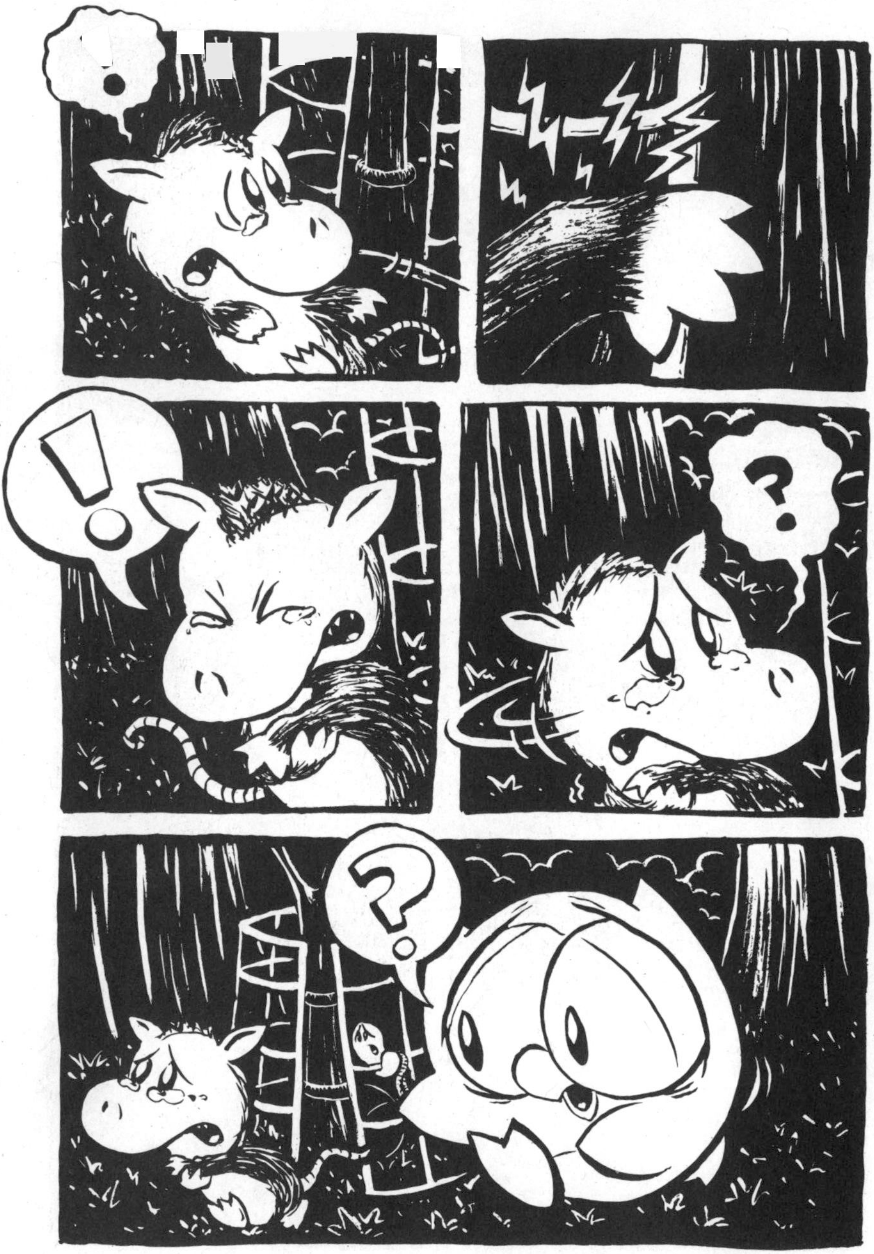
!
?
?

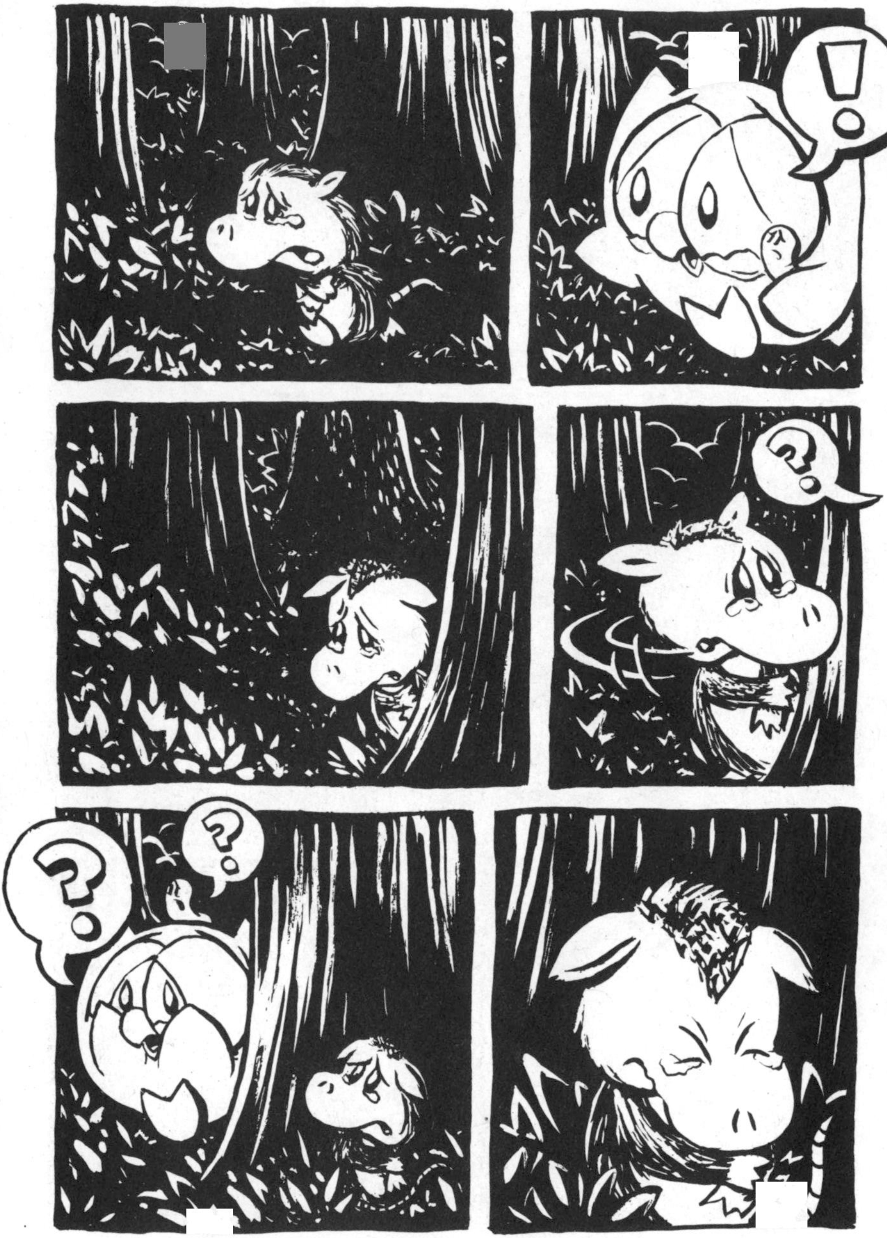
!
?
?
?

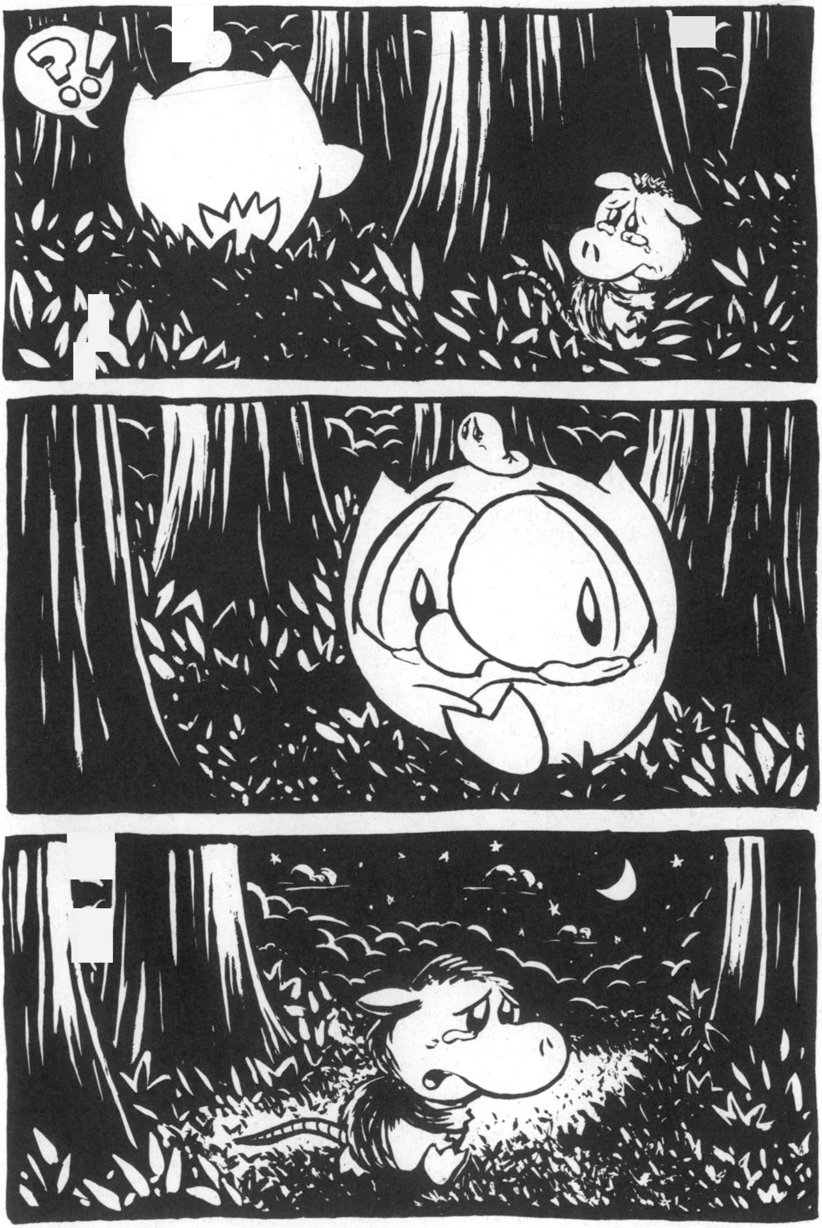
?!

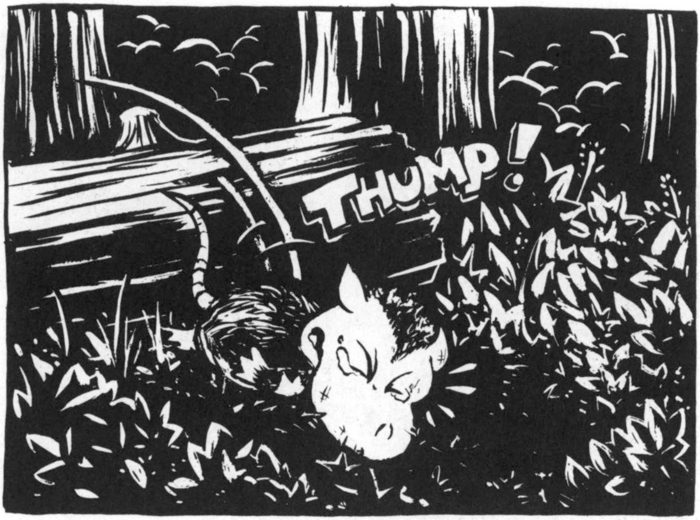
THUMP!

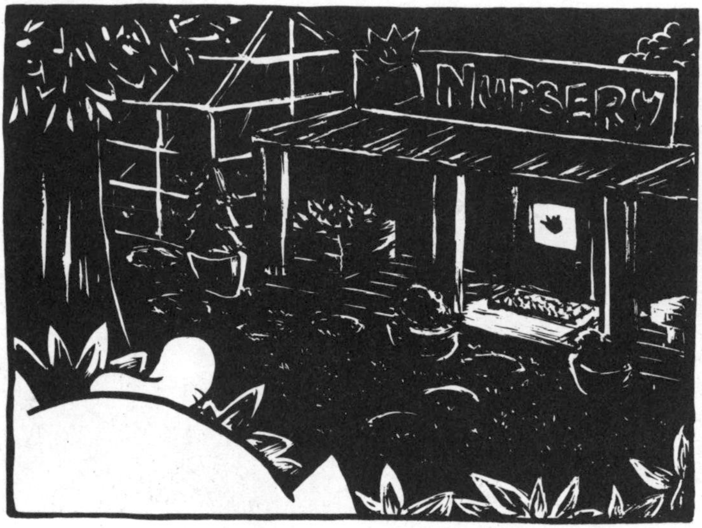
NURSERY

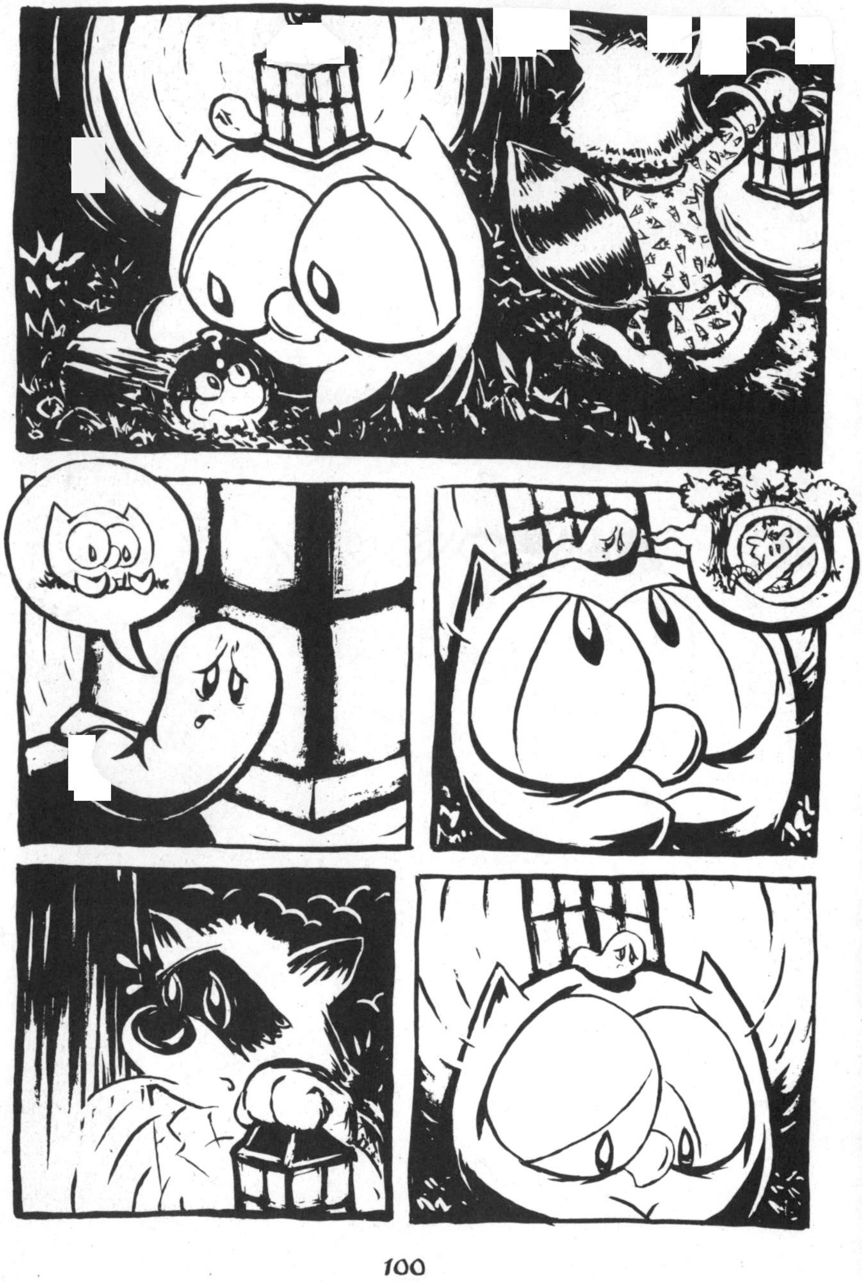

101

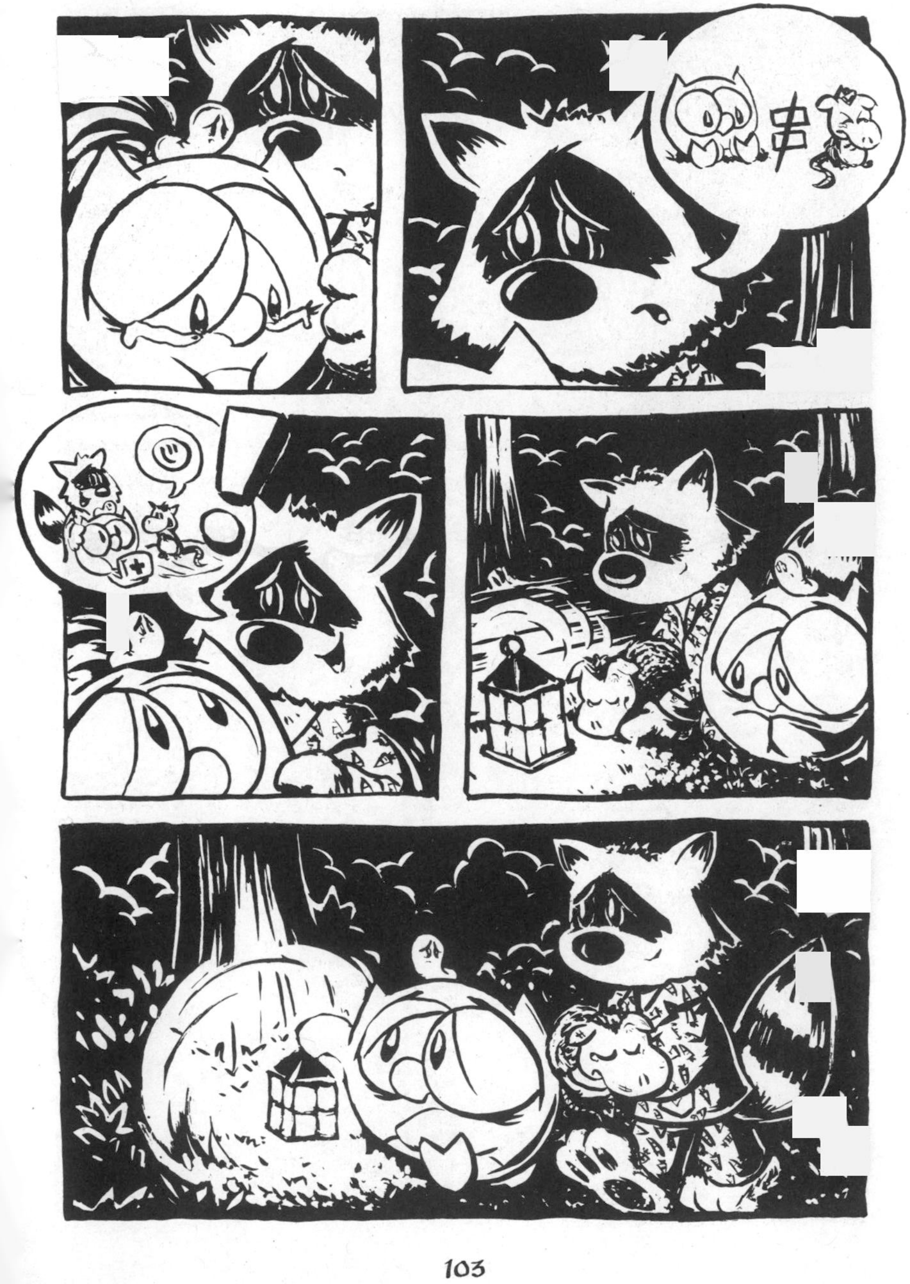

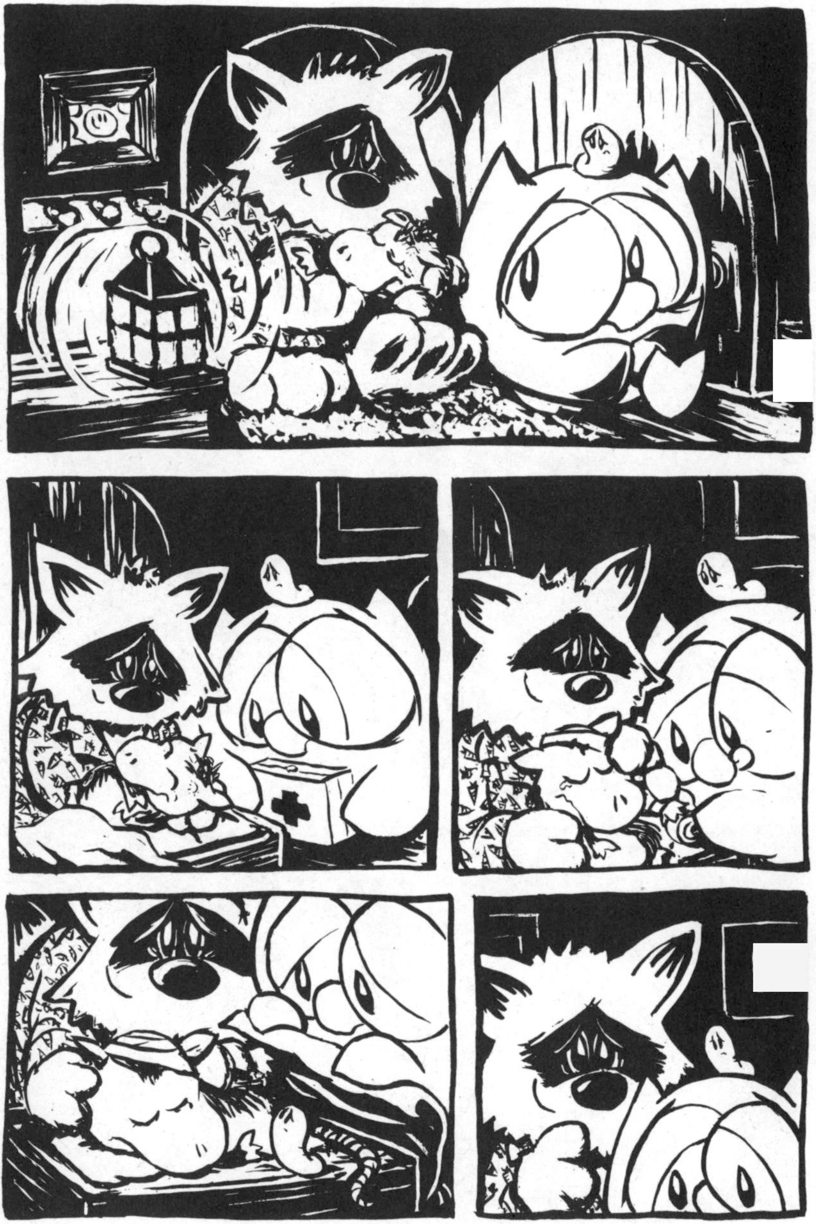

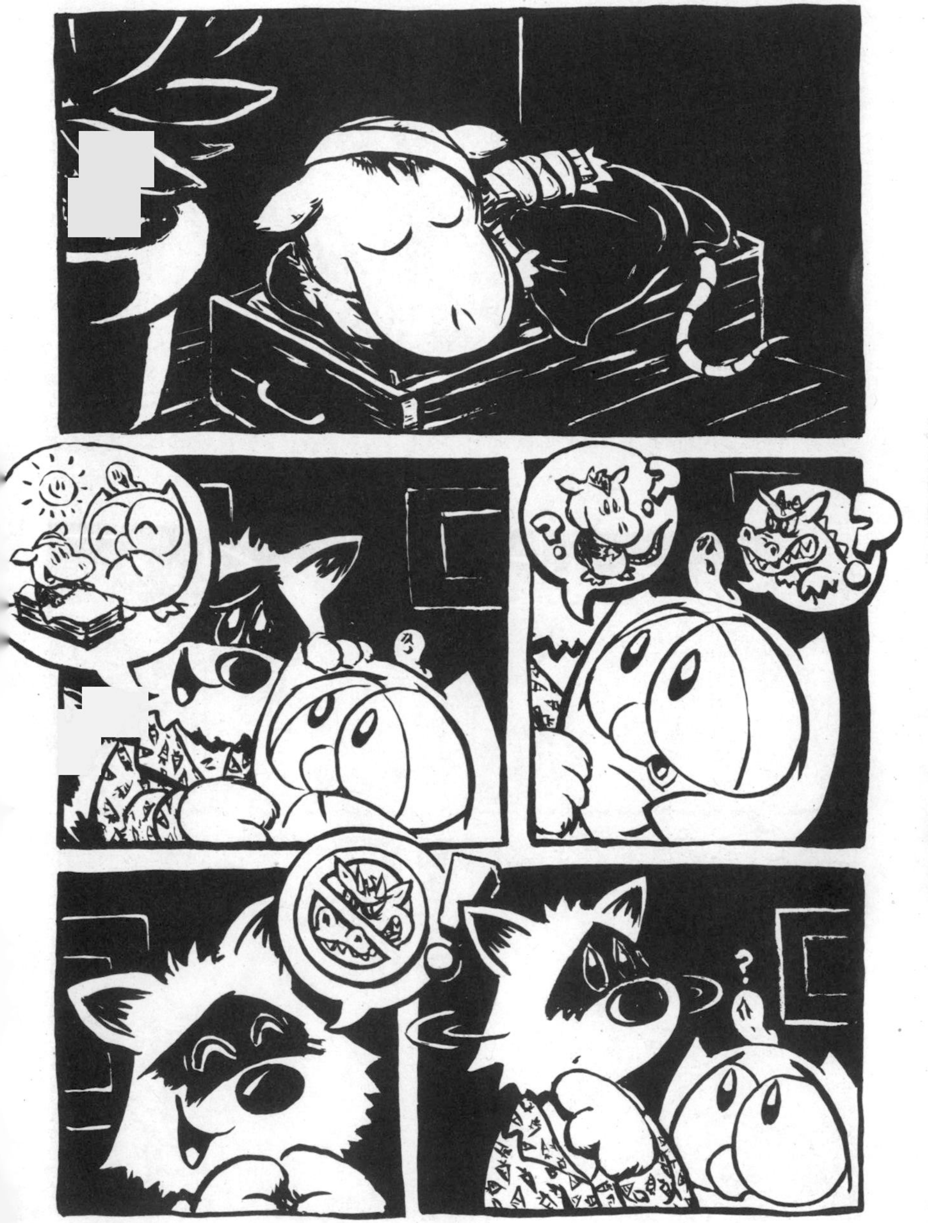

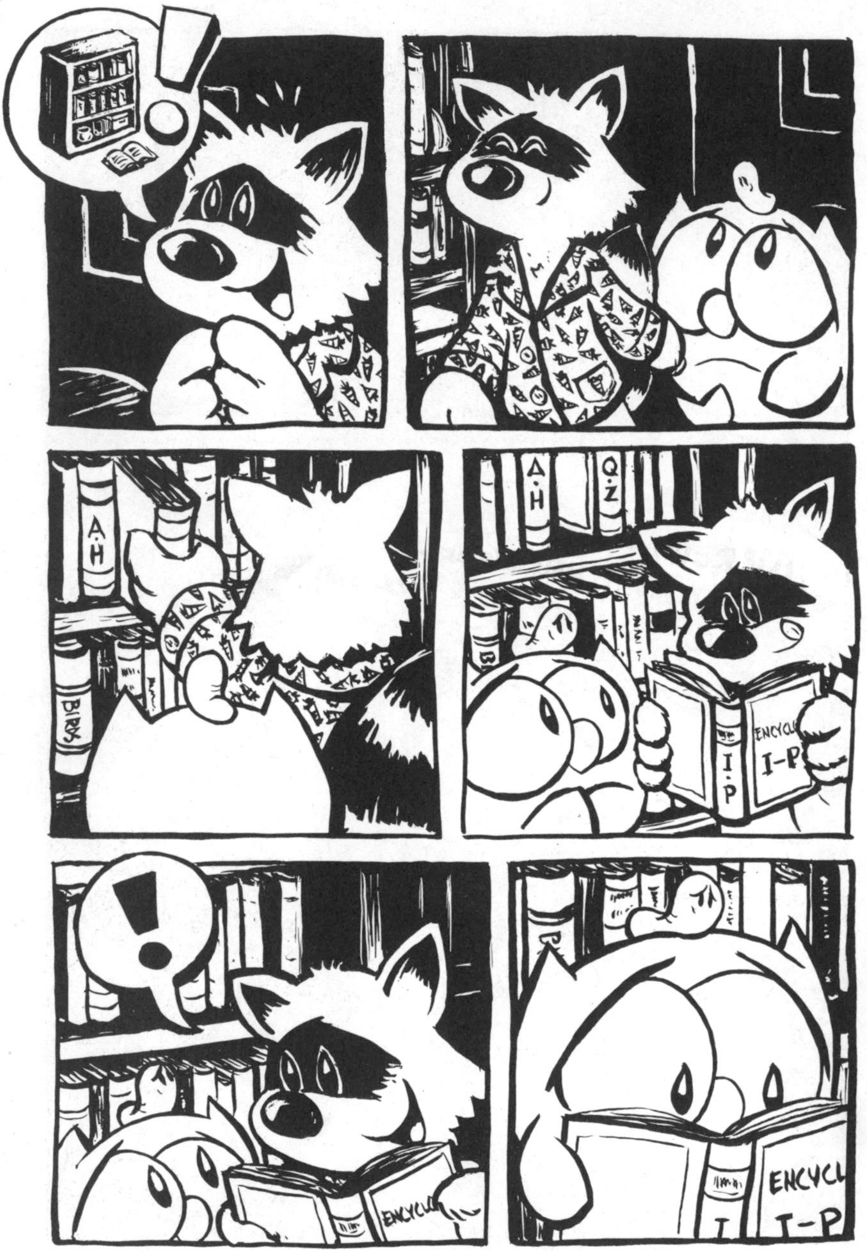
!
A·H
Q·Z
BIRDS
ENCYCL
I-P
!
ENCYCL
ENCYCL
I-P

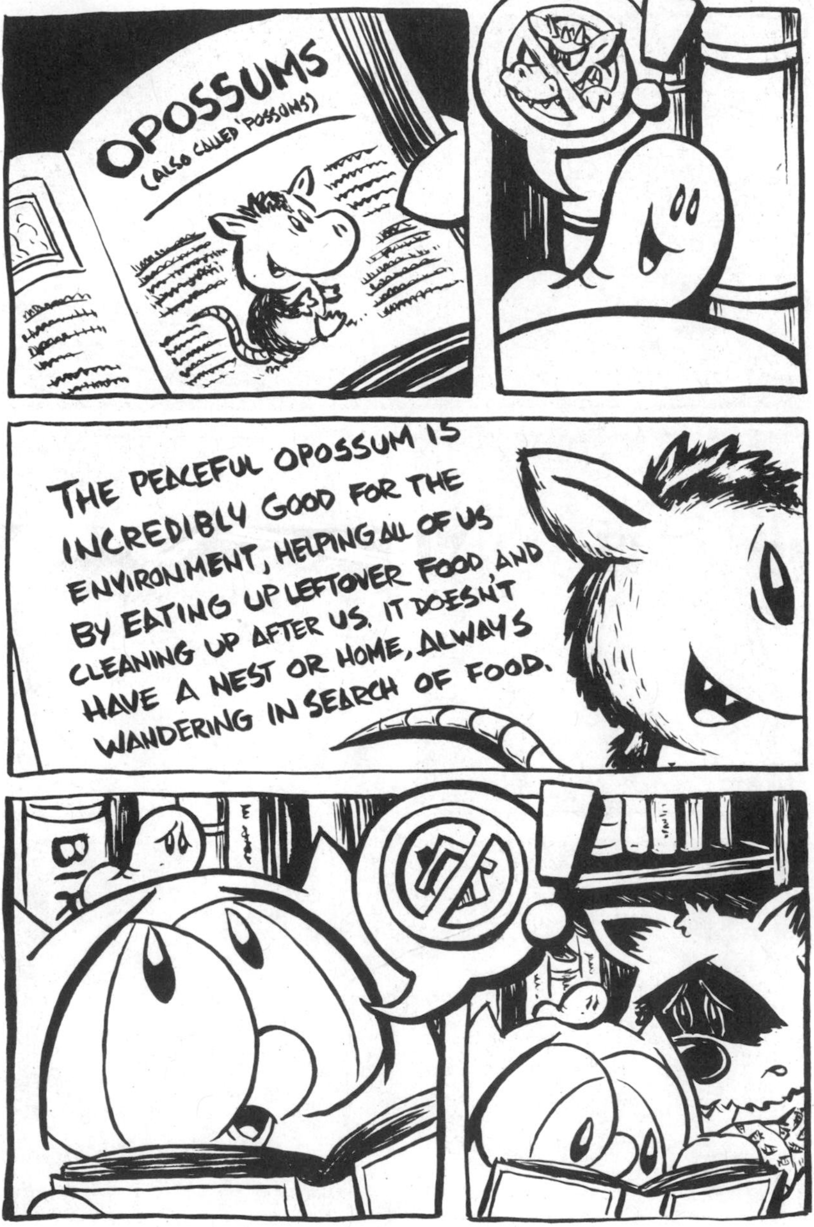
OPOSSUMS
(ALSO CALLED 'POSSUMS)
THE PEACEFUL OPOSSUM IS INCREDIBLY GOOD FOR THE ENVIRONMENT, HELPING ALL OF US BY EATING UP LEFTOVER FOOD, AND CLEANING UP AFTER US. IT DOESN'T HAVE A NEST OR HOME, ALWAYS WANDERING IN SEARCH OF FOOD.

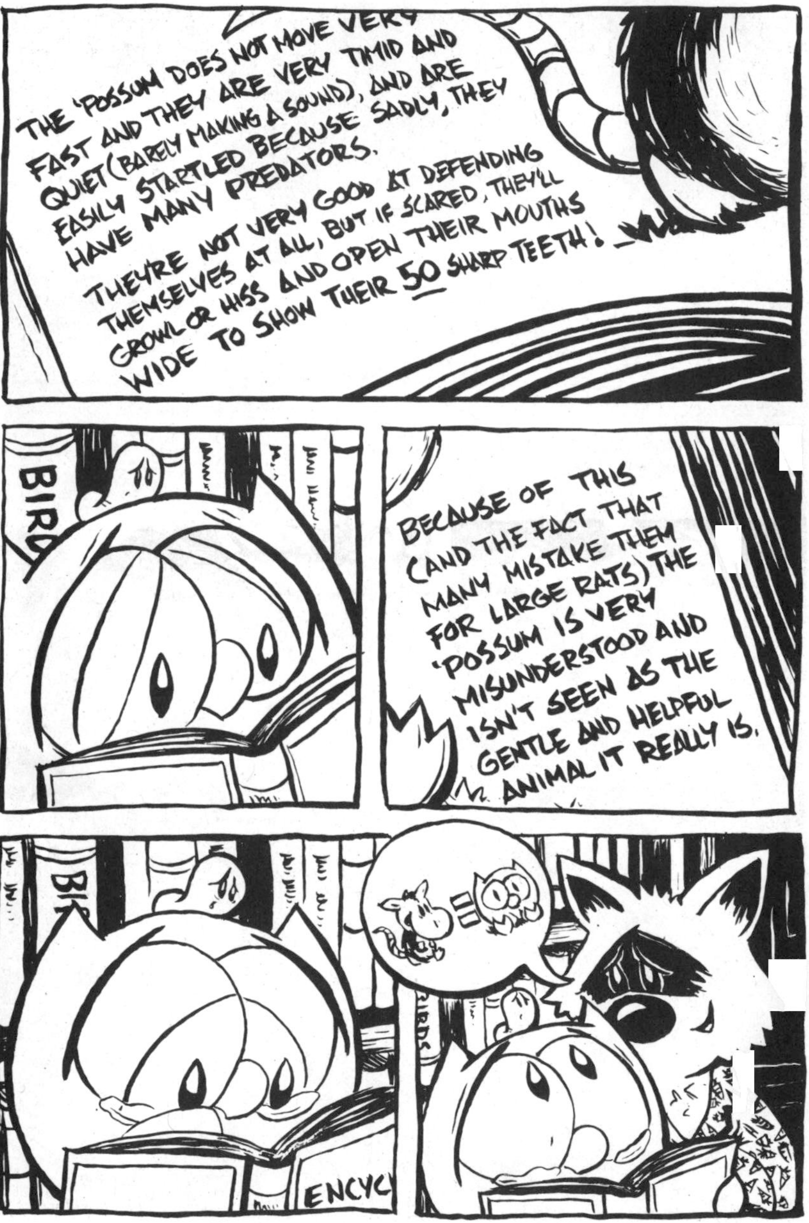
THE 'POSSUM DOES NOT MOVE VERY FAST AND THEY ARE VERY TIMID AND QUIET (BARELY MAKING A SOUND), AND ARE EASILY STARTLED BECAUSE SADLY, THEY HAVE MANY PREDATORS.
THEY'RE NOT VERY GOOD AT DEFENDING THEMSELVES AT ALL, BUT IF SCARED, THEY'LL GROWL OR HISS AND OPEN THEIR MOUTHS WIDE TO SHOW THEIR 50 SHARP TEETH!
BECAUSE OF THIS (AND THE FACT THAT MANY MISTAKE THEM FOR LARGE RATS) THE 'POSSUM IS VERY MISUNDERSTOOD AND ISN'T SEEN AS THE GENTLE AND HELPFUL ANIMAL IT REALLY IS.
BIRDS

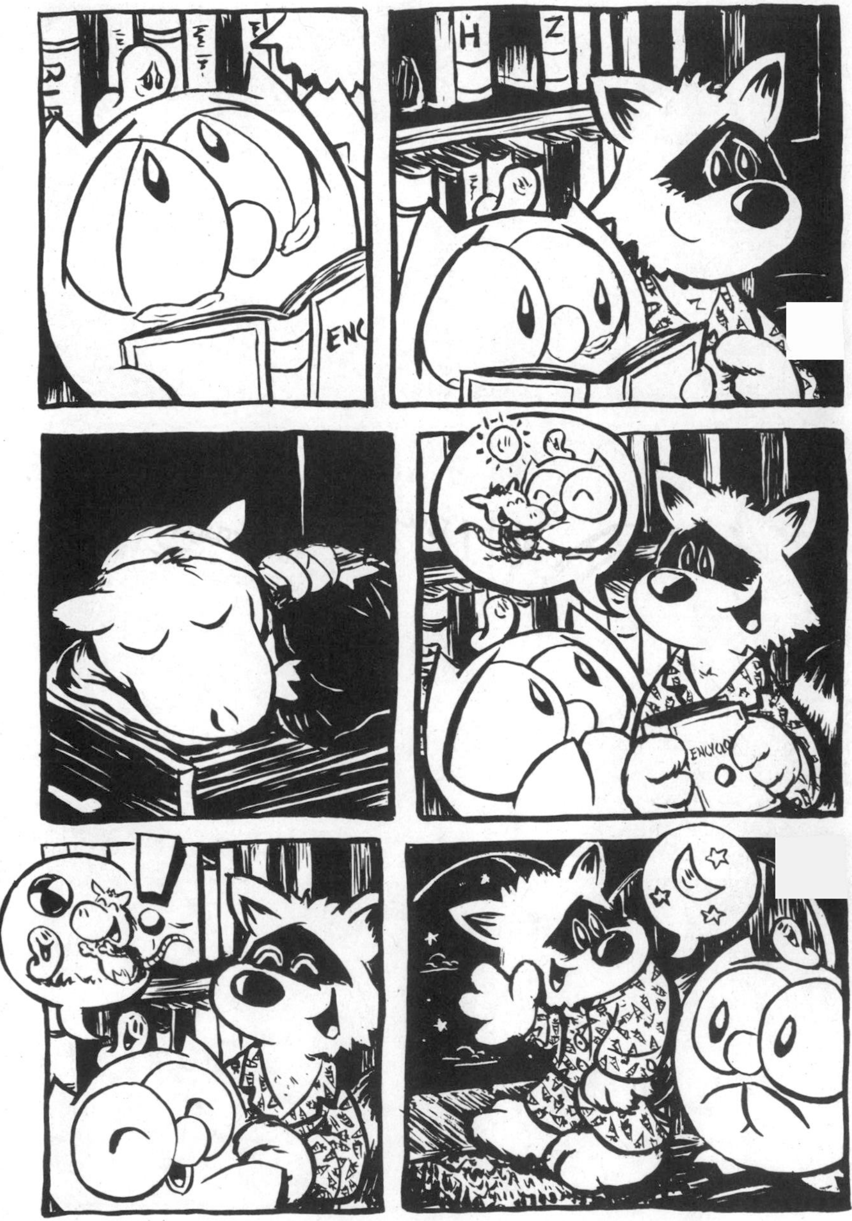
ENC
H
Z
ENCYCLO
!

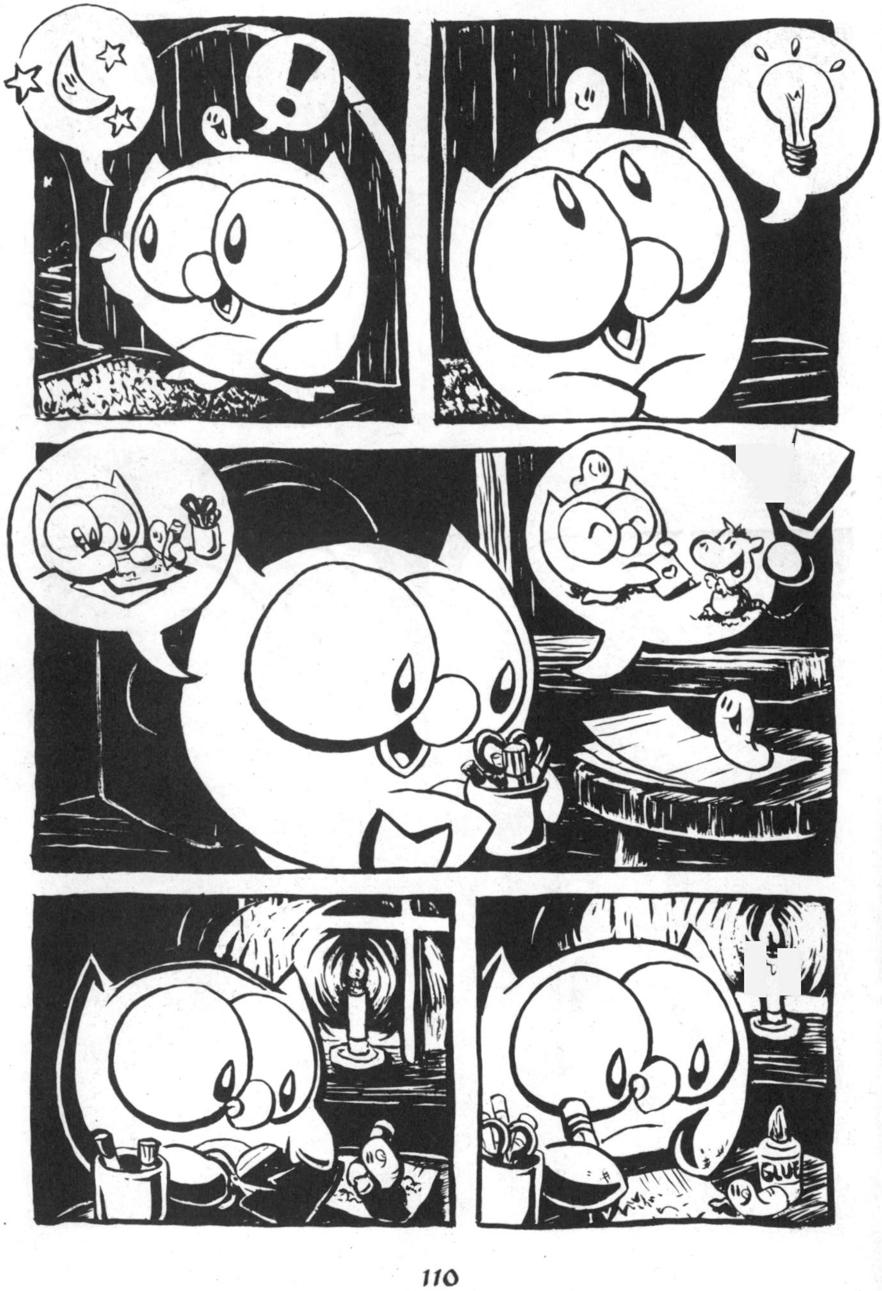
!
GLUE

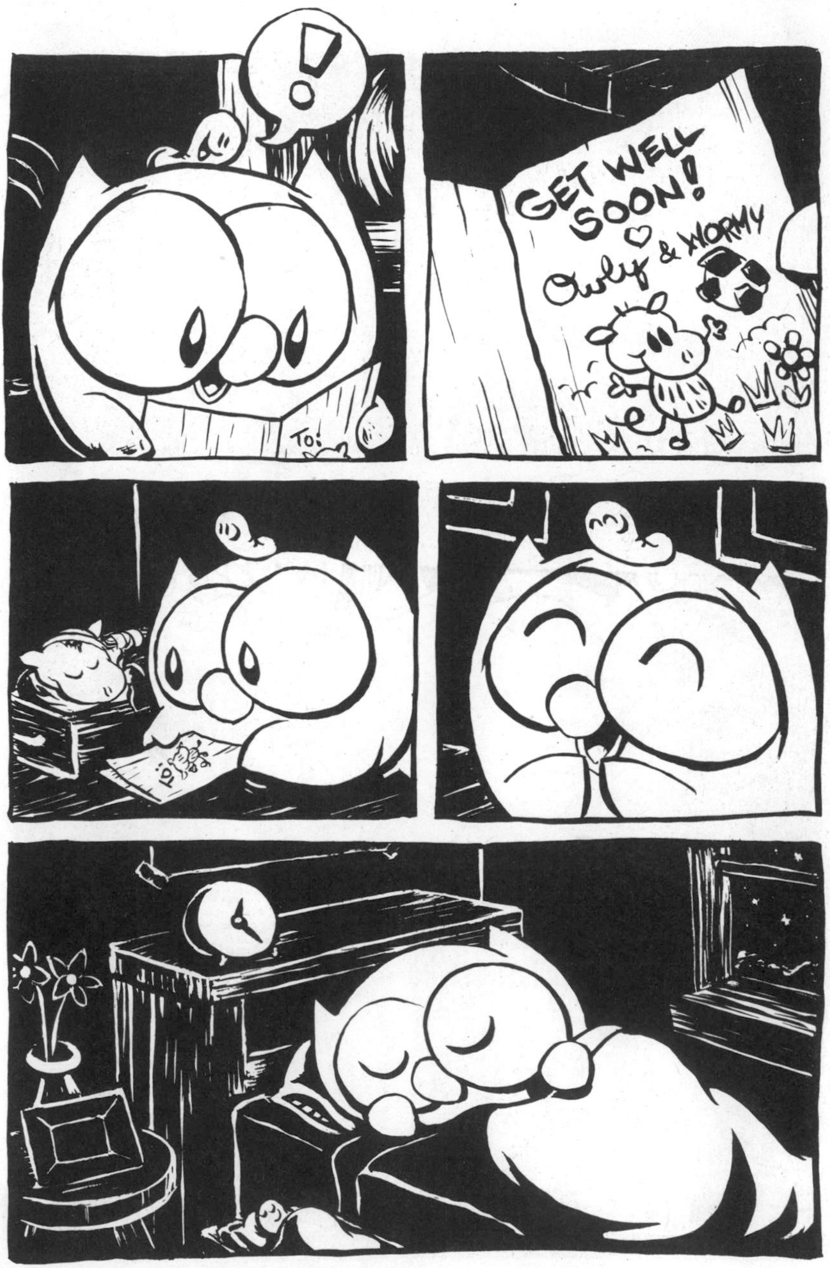
!
TO:
GET WELL SOON!
Owly & WORMY
TO:

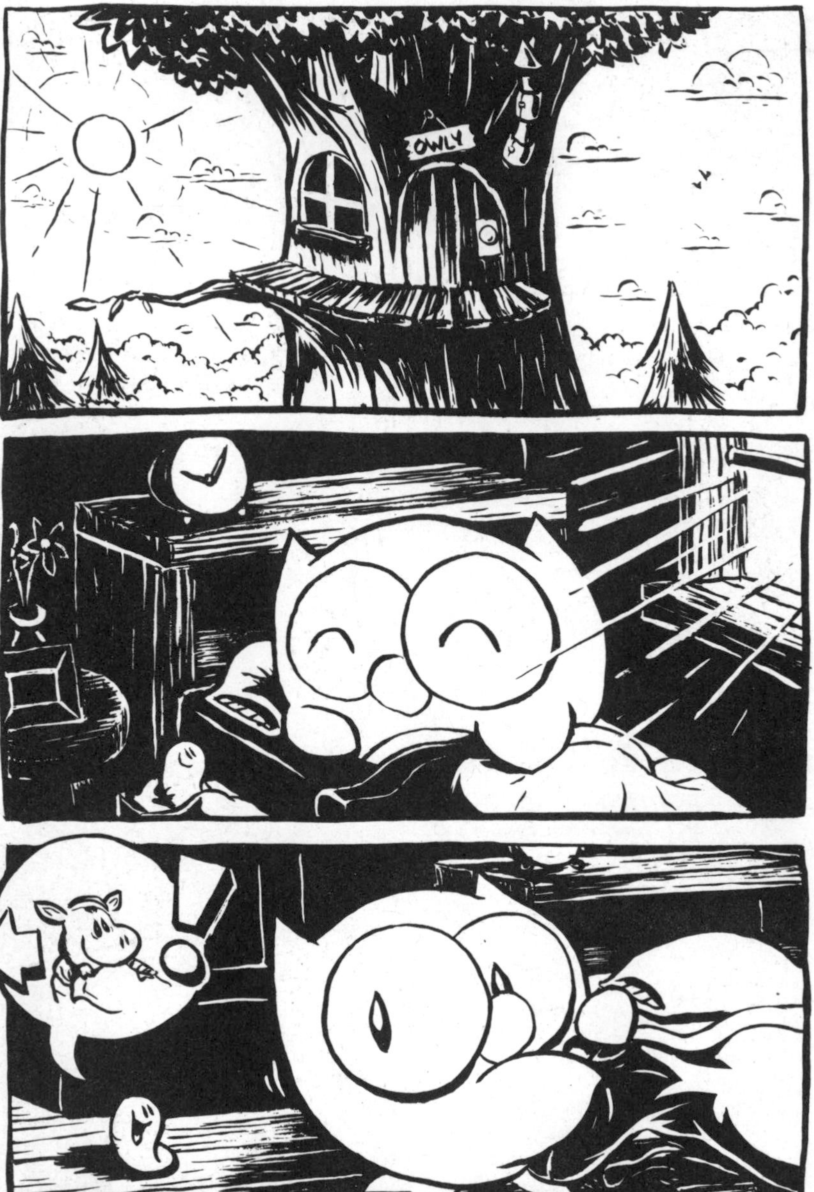
OWLY

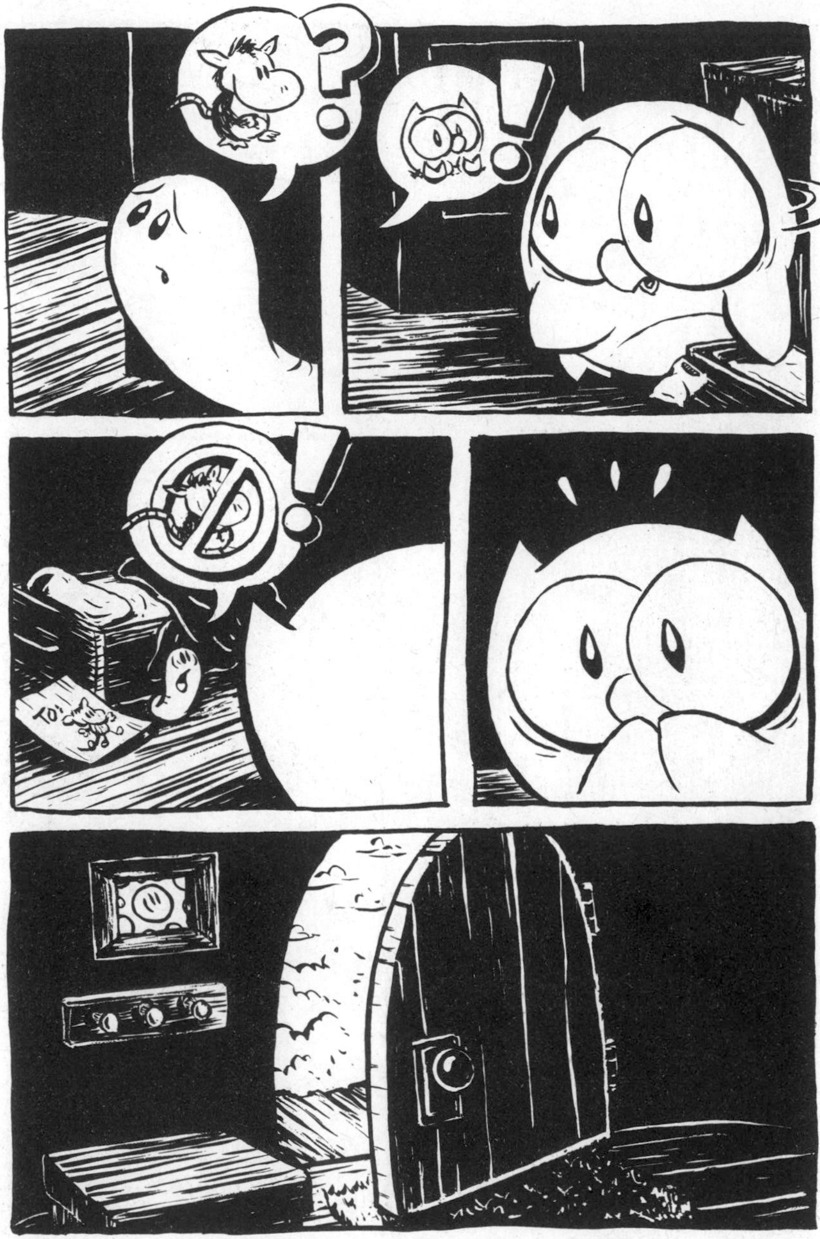
TO:

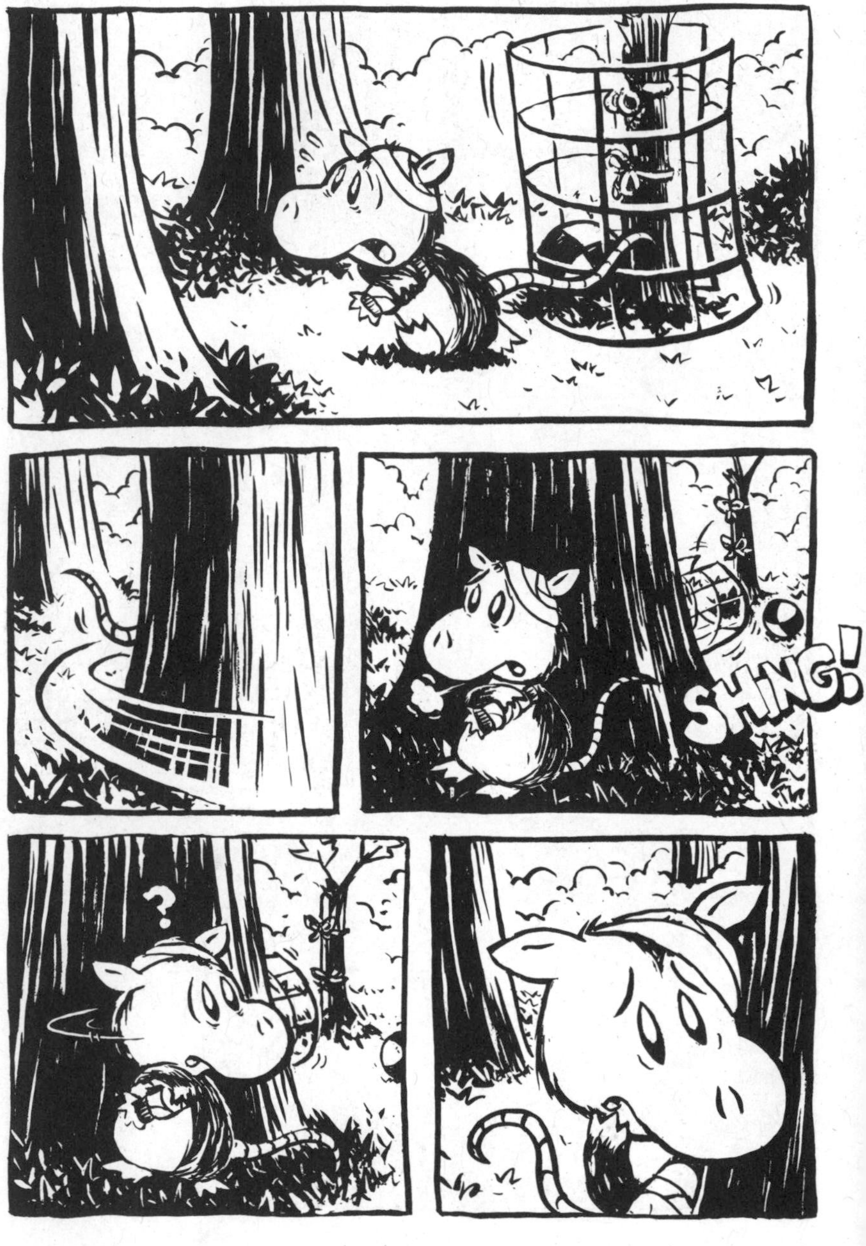
SHING!
?

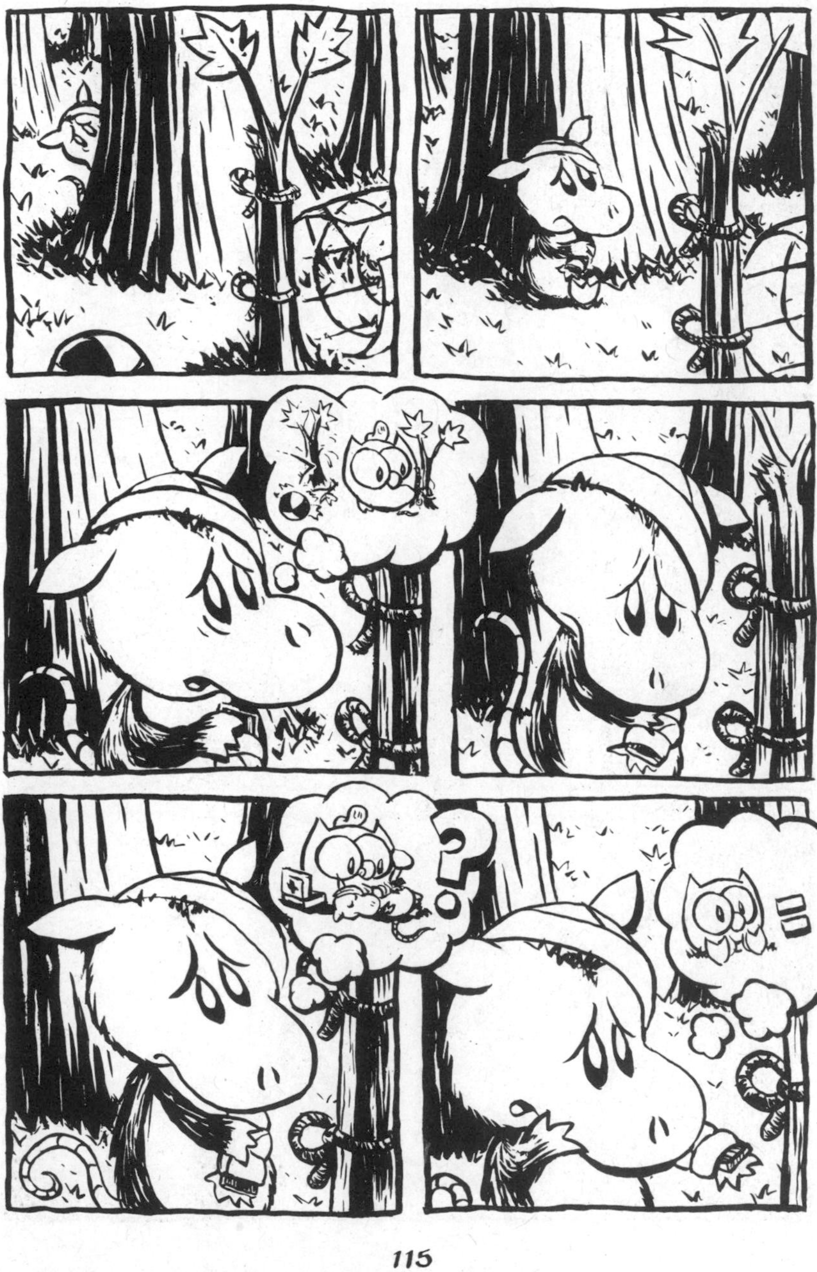

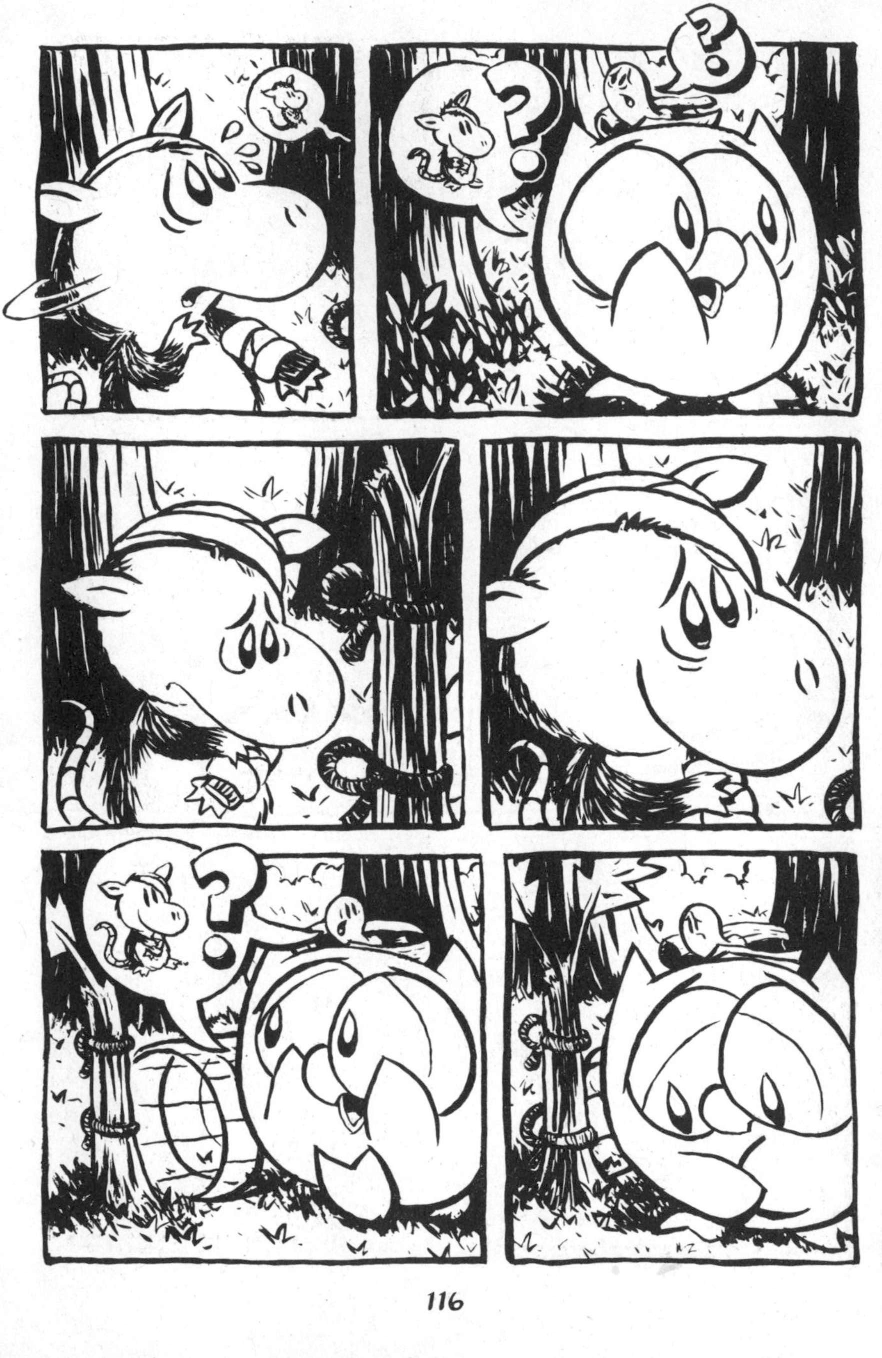
?
?
?

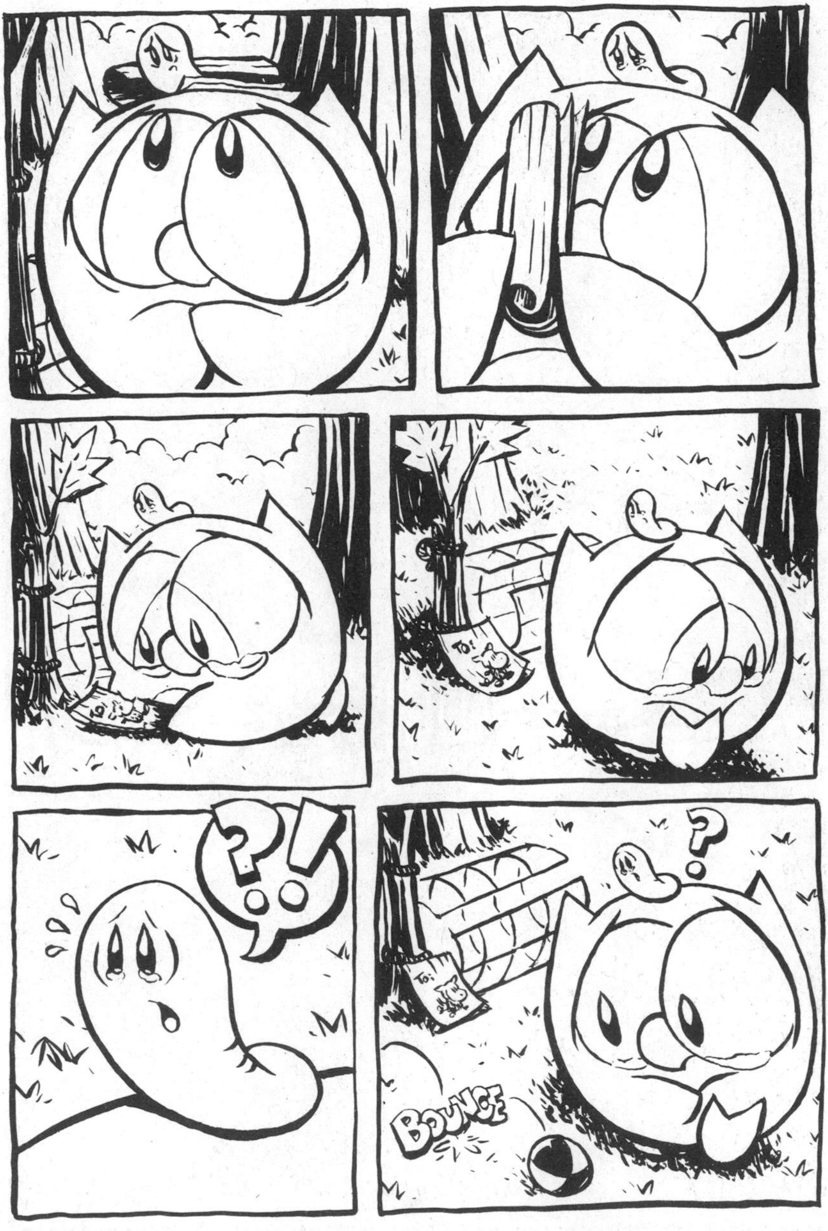
To:
?!
To:
?
To:
BOUNCE

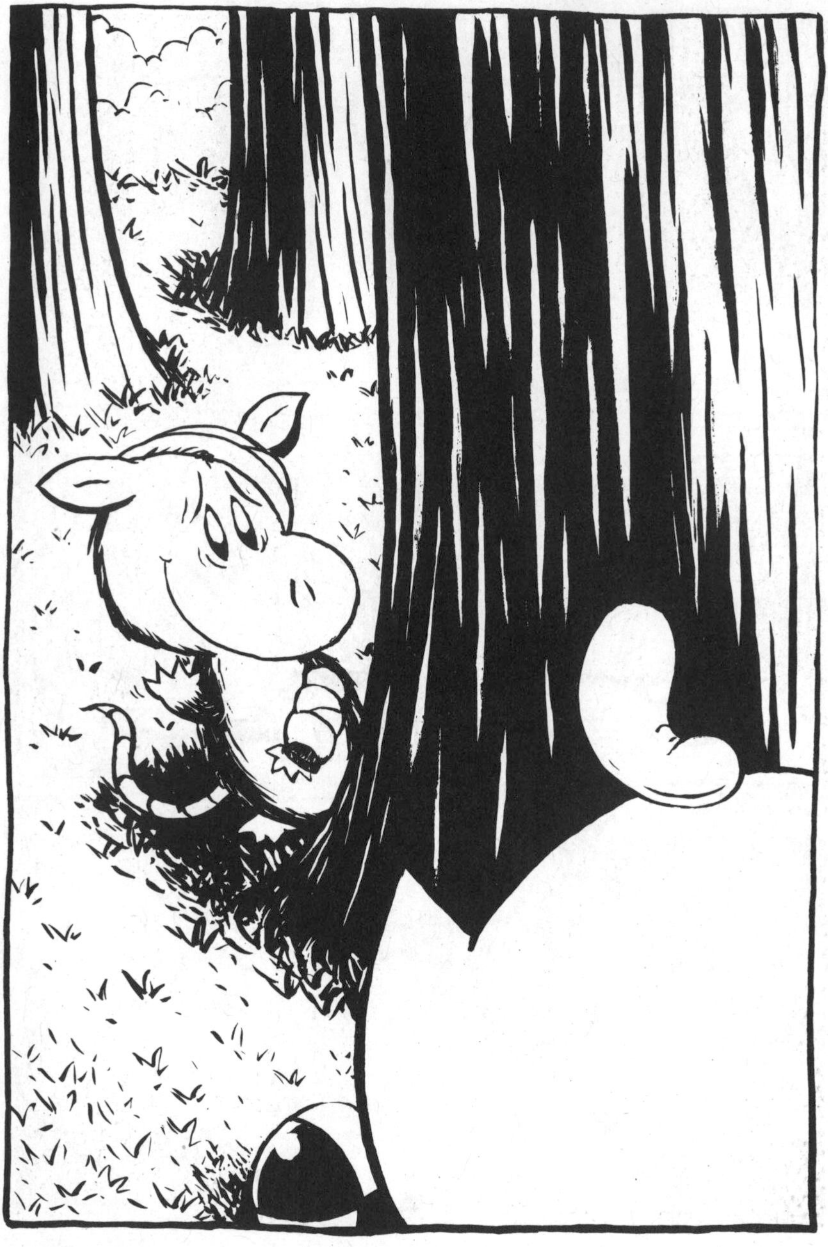

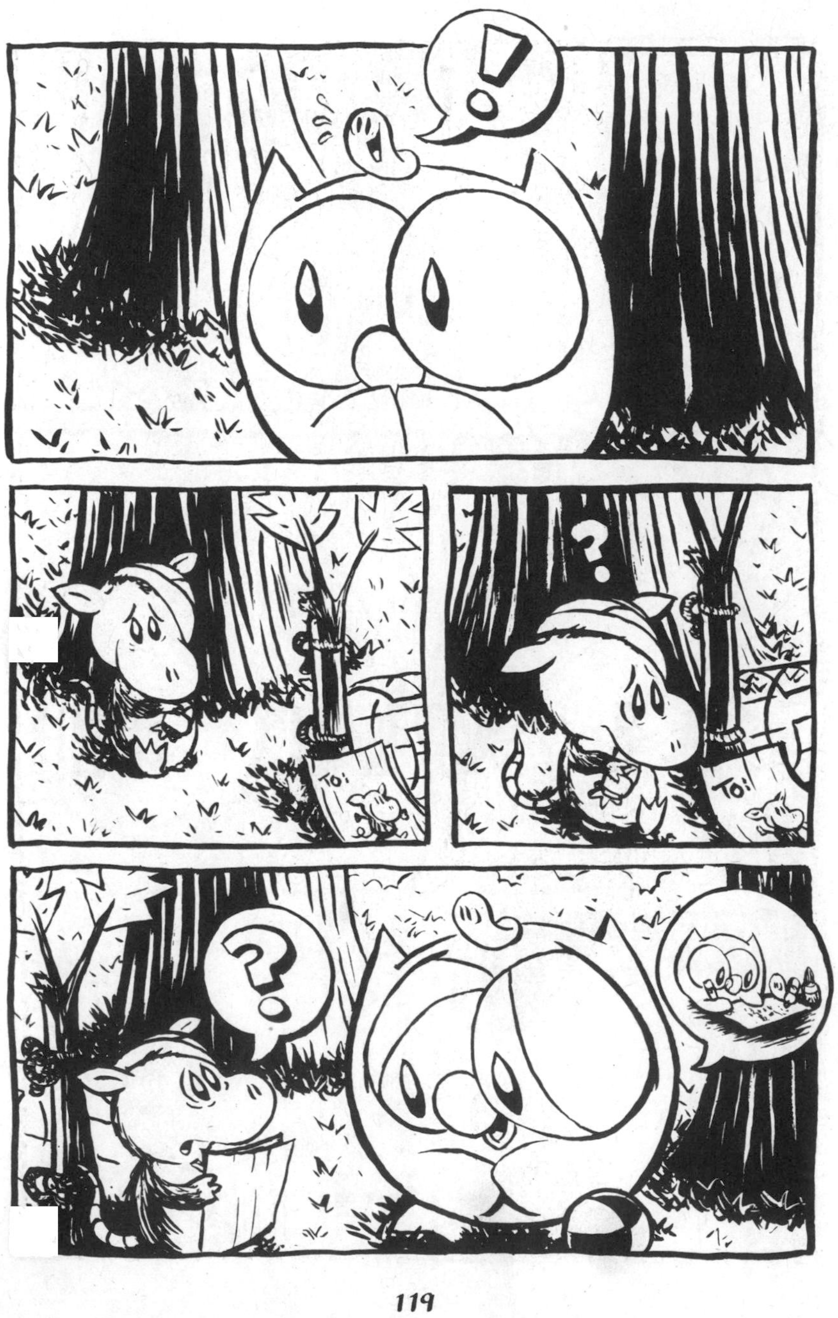
!
TO:
?
TO:
?

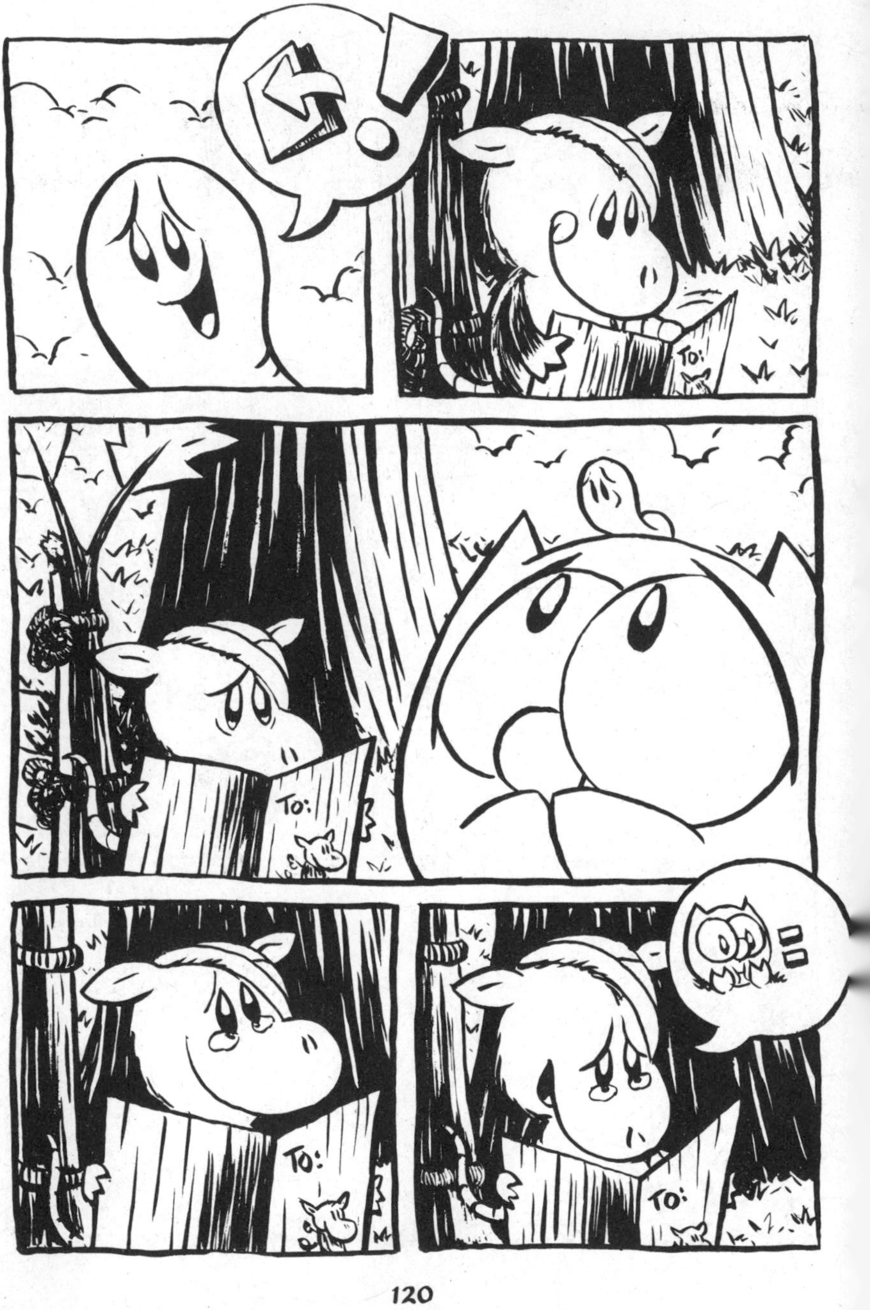
To:
To:
To:
To:

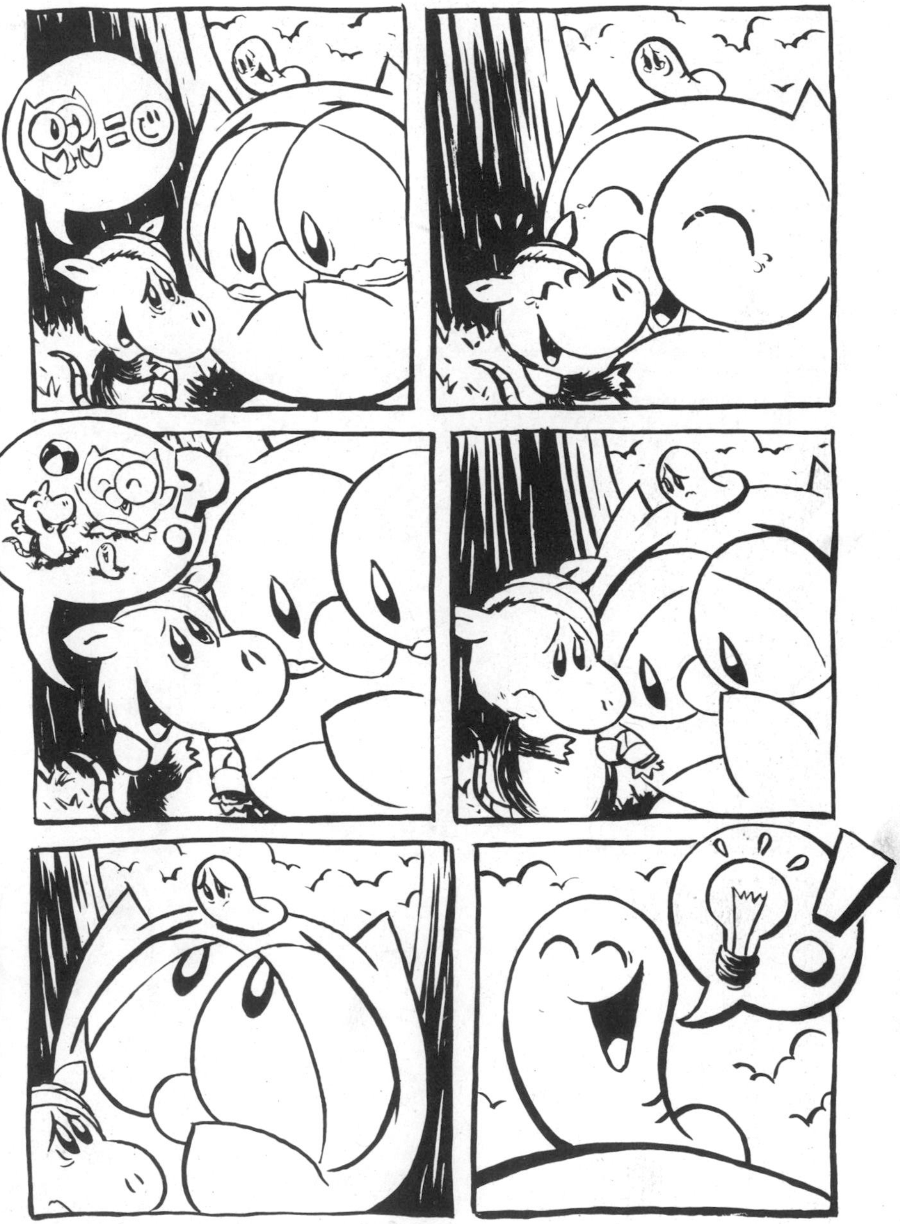

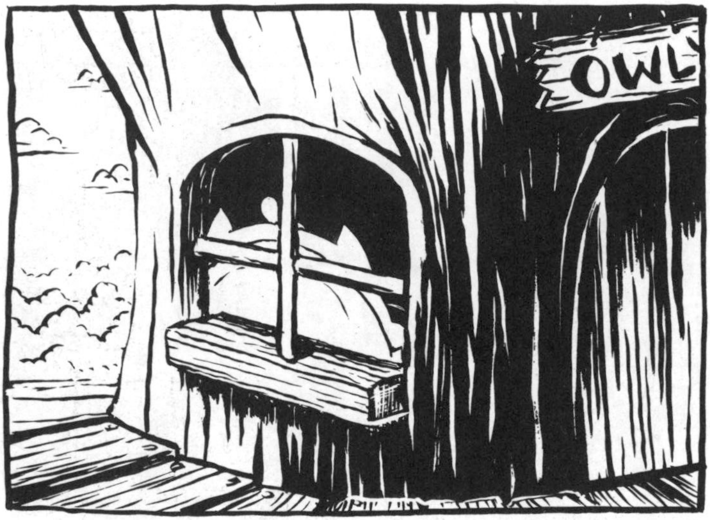
OWL

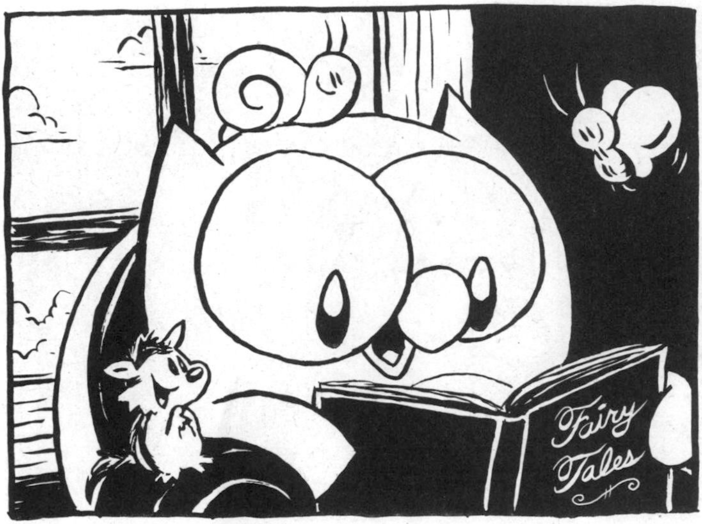
Fairy Tales

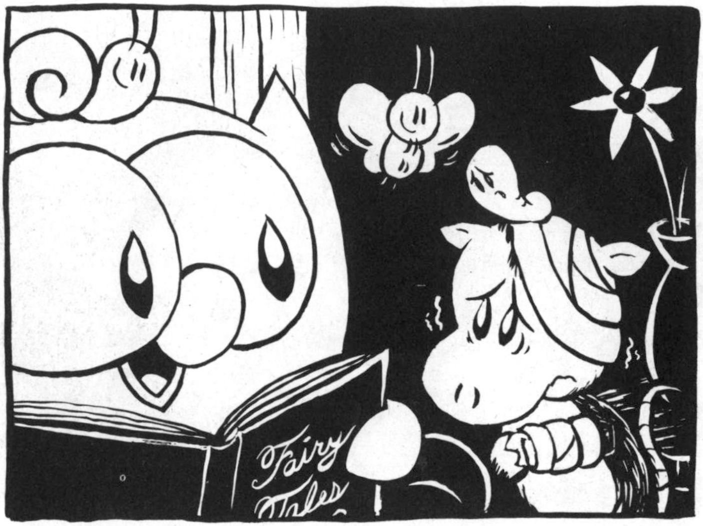
Fairy Tales

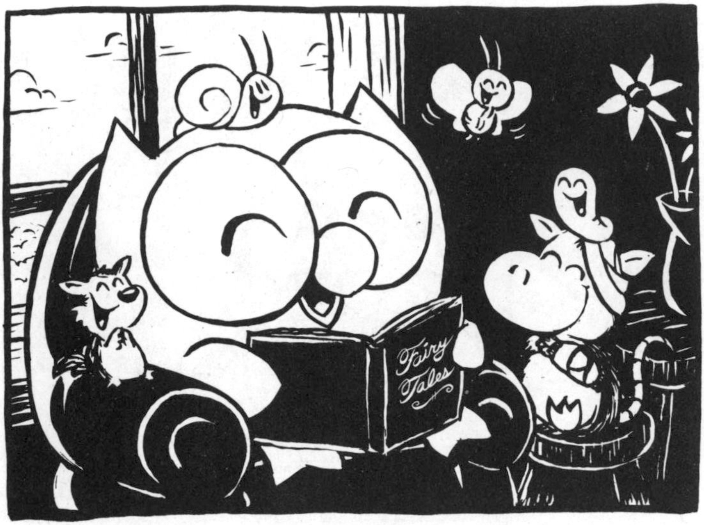
Fairy Tales

THE END!

The brave Sir Possey defends
Princess Flutter from the scary
Wormy, Scampy, and Snaily dragon!

(¨

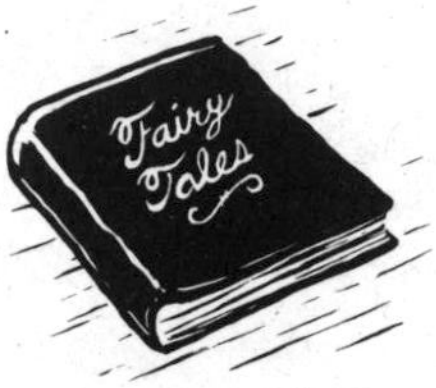
Fairy
Tales

MORE OWLY BOOKS!

OWLY: VOLUME ONE,
THE WAY HOME & THE BITTERSWEET SUMMER

ISBN 10: 1-891830-62-7 , ISBN 13: 978-1-891830-62-4

OWLY: VOLUME TWO,
JUST A LITTLE BLUE

ISBN 10: 1-891830-64-3 , ISBN 13: 978-1-891830-64-8

OWLY: VOLUME THREE,
FLYING LESSONS

ISBN 10: 1-891830-76-7 , ISBN 13: 978-1-891830-76-1

: OWLY @ MAC.COM

: OWLY & ANDY RUNTON
5502 EAST WIND DR.
LILBURN, GA 30047-6410
U.S.A.

WWW.ANDYRUNTON.COM

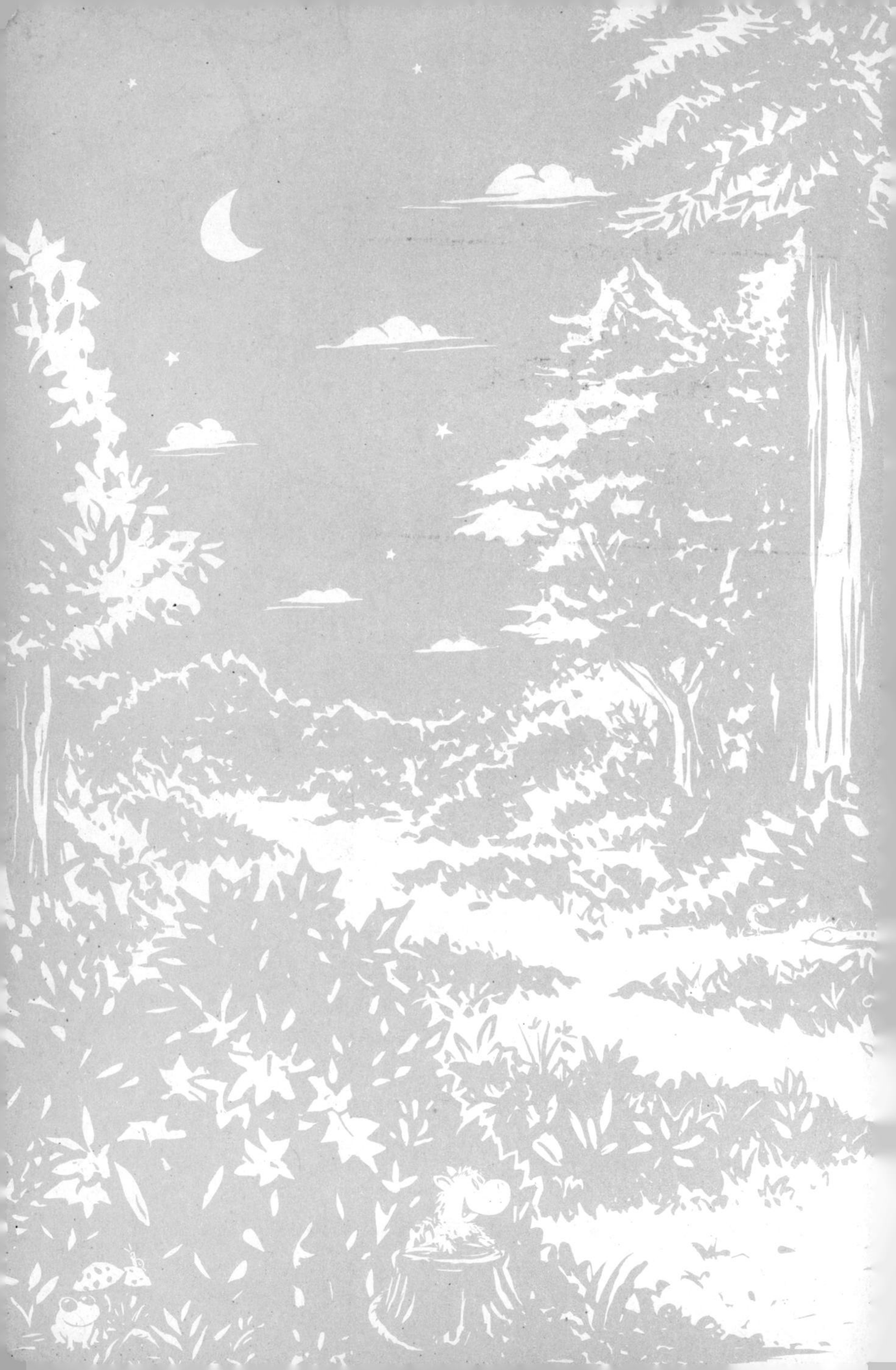